Three in One

Also by Ray Clift and published by Ginninderra Press

Fiction

The Journey of Hamlyn Baylis Wells

Always In Denial

Smithy's Cupboard

Shaken & Stirred

Shalom Samuel

The Last Journey of Hamlin Baylis Wells

She Walks the Line

Non-fiction

Maybe Blue Ghosts

It's a Fine Line

Cops, Crooks, Courts & Spooks

Ray Clift

Three in One

Acknowledgements

My gratitude goes primarily to Stephen Matthews of
Ginninderra Press and his partner Brenda Eldridge.

To Ann for providing the space in order to write…
To Kerry and Jo, my daughters, for their encouragement.
To good friends Jim and Irene Davey for their careful honest evaluation,
and Peter and Barbara Shepherd, Silvio and Rose Belotti and Chris Sharp.
To Phil and Vicki Brophy. To Don and Lorraine Hay.

To Ken Vincent and Sharon Kernot, Gary MacRae and
the other members of North Eastern Writers Inc.

To the many SA police and sheriffs officers I knew.

This edition published 2015 by
GINNINDERRA PRESS
PO Box 3461 Port Adelaide SA 5015
www.ginninderrapress.com.au

Contents

Always in Denial

Prologue

As he hesitantly made his way along the darkened street, alarm sprouted in John Taylor's mind like a patch of newly sown bean seeds.

His mind was crowded with an intermix of thoughts, of sin and evil, which were spliced with expectations of what awaited him at the end of the journey. He knew he was not free from sin and he pondered on evil and how it had wormed its way into the crucible of his soul. The vivid dreams he had spoken over the years had provided no answers to perplexing questions such as 'Are we born evil or are we held in its claws? Are those claws enticing to some of us who might not be able to resist them?'

The drab darkness of the street on the misty night heightened his innermost fears and he jumped at the sound of a nearby train whistle blowing a mournful dirge which seemed to cut through the atmosphere.

Dispossessed people lay strewn about, edged into the grey-black vacant doorways which gave some assurance to the unlucky few that their secret life in their secret world would remain hidden at least for one more night. Some of them had made tragic choices; some of them had missed a pivotal moment; while others had simply fallen through the cracks. However and whatever, they were lumped together and labelled as insignificant or, worse, 'a waste of oxygen' by some people who gave no thought to the circumstances of the so-called ferals.

John had empathy for the dark huddles with their sour smell flooding the air, yet it was a passing emotion, flowing along like a fast stream and leaving his mind within seconds. Just like his father used to say he should, he picked up his feet as he passed along, watchful but unthreatened.

He had built up a good life with a nice home in a leafy suburb of Adelaide which was far away from the world of the darkened street. He was married to an immaculate wife with good connections, a social worker with a propensity to undergo regular botox injections. The child with whom they were blessed was living in Switzerland with a sound engineer and rumours of marriage were in the air. Yet hidden desires lurked within him. He had worked hard to suppress the dual sexuality which had troubled his life but the shame of trying to hide sexual abuse survived, slowly simmering like sea bubbling on the shore.

And then the tempting gold-edged card arrived in the mail.

John fingered the card on his approach to the address. He recalled the words inside: 'See me for a good time.'

His thoughts were turning over and over like an empty carton blown about in the wind, powerless to resist the forces of nature.

He had passed the point of self-control and quickened his pace towards the old doorway covered in red graffiti with its number: 666. His first chakra was expanding at the base of his spine. Urged on by raging lust, his curiosity had reached an alarming level.

The door squeaked with the sound of neglect as he pushed it inwards. He was confronted with a long dark passage which was devoid of lighting, and he took three hesitant steps inside, into the labyrinth, with his back pressed flat against the wall. His scalp was tingling in the oppressive shadows.

He inched along with his hands stretched out, fingers extended, expecting someone or something to grasp his hands at any moment. His breath was coming in short gasps and his stomach was heaving in and out like a child's bladder in the playground.

He saw a door and he whispered to a God of long ago, 'Thank you.'

He shoved the door open in one almighty heave; blazing lights blinded his eyes. He blinked and focused into a sight of happy people. His wife stood in front holding a giant cake with many candles, the appearance of a smile on her carbolicly scrubbed face. He studied her face as he closed the gap between them and in the moment when he entered her space, she turned her lips away. Her eyes revealed a mixture of sadness and triumph. He bent to kiss her cheek and in that instant he knew: she had found his secret.

She led the chorus as everyone sang, 'Happy birthday to John. Happy birthday to John.'

1

John

The photos of my family were preserved inside an old Crompton's soap box, the one with the portrait of a child with a cheeky face, rosy cheeks and twinkling eyes which said she was an old soul, as the northern England folk were fond of saying. Her almost naked body with the nappy hanging down showed a child in good health, which belied the times when children died of a range of diseases.

Within the box lay an assortment of old, dried, well fingered items which were mixed in amongst the lingering odours of camphor flakes, dried lavender leaves and some rosemary (for remembrance); there was a compass which looked as if it came off an ancient ship, a knife and an array of sepia photos. The photos were mainly of bearded males with top hats and walking canes. Ladies were scattered amongst the serious unsmiling men and they wore high-necked blouses, long flowing skirts and wide-brimmed hats. Perhaps it had been raining when the photos were taken, as the women all held opened umbrellas.

The photo of the dead man inside a coffin always gripped me and held my focus when I was able to sneak in and examine the family treasures. His hands were clasped across his chest and the skin on close examination was like a dried banana skin. His eyes were closed and there was a man dressed like an undertaker pointing at the corpse, almost like a big game hunter with his prized trophy. So this is it – death…before and after, I would surmise.

Death seemed to follow our family like a lady in waiting. I was intrigued by death – not my own death, but that of my older half-brother Albert, who had forced his uncontrolled lust upon me shortly after he came to live with us, when I was about eleven years of age. I imagined there would come a time when the stars were aligned; when I would be older, smarter and stronger and he would have a weak moment. Revenge would be bitter sweet.

Albert Garrison lived in a caravan at the rear of the giant block of land which our house stood on. He had come to our house after his wife, my Auntie Elsie, died. Elsie of the frog-like eyes which bolted out of her head like a surprised meerkat – like organ stops, my usually kind mother would say. She spoke with some spite, because Albert, her first born, was her favourite and she would not listen to anything negative about him. When it came to Albert, she was always in denial.

Elsie's eyes looked even wider because of her permanently high, arched eyebrows, plucked almost to oblivion, which must have been a painful nightly ritual. She seemed to be constantly anticipating an answer to a question or a riddle. When she spoke, her mouth exposed an array of pointed yellow teeth which clattered between the moments when her small pointed tongue darted out like a blue tongue lizard. I wondered if her very busy tongue and the stammering caused the laboured speech patterns, which were almost like a truck changing gears.

'She won't make old bones,' Dad said, and within a few years he was proved right.

Elsie's best feature was her thick blonde curly hair, which was usually worn high like Lana Turner until the onset of the cancer which took her life. Her treasured locks began to fall, slowly at first, then great clumps came away till a wig was found for her. The large wig fell across her eyebrows and at times the poor woman looked like an English sheepdog. Her normally high-pitched voice, which put out quick phrases with a silence to follow, just faded away. She became still and silent, withered and drained, clutching her large gold cross right till the time when she gave a final puff and passed on, with Albert weeping crocodile tears and Mum praying for her soul.

Her funeral was a quiet affair, with her beloved priest muttering a monologue of pointless scriptures delivered in a half sloshed Irish accent, coupled with a smoky whisky smell from his breath which flooded the coffin on his right. An equally drunken Irish fiddler gave us a squeaky rendition of 'The Mountains of Morne' as if he had just come from an Irish pub on a Friday night, and she was carried out by a group of burly men in black suits to her final resting place (until her resurrection from the grave, which she firmly believed would come).

Albert got to work within a few days, busying himself by removing any sign that poor Elsie had passed by for a brief time on this planet. He removed all of her precious symbols, the lambs held by Jesus, Jesus blessing the fish, the last supper and – the final blasphemy – Jesus bleeding on the cross. He threw them all, plus her Bible (which Mum finally chastised him for), into the besser-block incinerator which held pride of place along with the Hills hoist clothes line at the rear of the rented Blair Athol house in the northern areas of Adelaide. The cardboard boxes all went up to heaven in a smokey musty-smelling haze.

We lived two streets away. I was born there in 1940 when Australia was at war. Mum loved her garden and was constantly digging, planting and pulling up any weeds which dared to survive. A wide-brimmed hat adorned her head, though protection from the sun was unnecessary because she had inherited a ruddy complexion from her Yorkshire bloodline. She wore shoes with inner soles which relieved her falling arches. Away from the garden she was a stylish mildly attractive woman, tall for her generation, with strong hands and long fingers, brown hair and brown eyes, and very slender. She always wore a gardenia (which she grew in profusion in acid-loving potting soil) to the dances with my Dad. And my, how they could dance.

She usually walked with her eyes peering at the ground in order to spot which ants were about (a great sign of rain, she said). Her fixed stare alerted her not to tread in dog poo and to avoid the old man's spit, which she hated. A very green-fingered person, she clipped cuttings from everywhere, and most survived. She was once caught by the head gardener at the Botanic Gardens with a handful of her favourites and was ordered to put them all back. She said that she felt like an ungrateful guest caught pinching the bath towels and she never went back to the gardens out of shame.

There were chrysanthemums and pom pom dahlias ready for Mother's Day, violets and hyacinths in spring, and the backyard was full of fruits, trees and vegetables. On the days when she caught the tram to the city markets, we would wait for her return. She would bound out of the Bib and Bub tram while it was still running, jumping off the running board and loaded to the gunwales with produce inside her home-made string bags. Moist newspapers were wrapped around a myriad of flowers and plants. She would stagger up the straight paved path, through the gate surrounding the seven-foot myrtle hedge, which she clipped twice a month

Stumbling through the vertical growth of the hollyhocks, irises and poppies in bloom and the plethora of other flowers in her front cottage garden, refusing all help from Dad, she would stop and smell the daphne and the hydrangeas in tubs under the wide bull-nosed veranda, brushing away the tendrils of the wisteria which adorned the veranda, and finally flopping in the big kitchen at the rear of the house.

Depending on the weather, she would slurp down a giant tablespoon full of milk emulsion, Saunders malt extract and Bonningtons Irish Moss and top it off by sucking on some butter menthols. Dad would make her a cup of Bushells tea and after dinner we would all listen to Mrs Obbs, Dad and Dave, Jack Davey and *Yes What*, which involved a bunch of cheeky kids baiting their schoolteacher. Two kids, Greenbottle and Bottomley, received the cane about ten times a day. And I knew some kids who were like that.

My parents never argued. Dad always agreed with her, as she was a great cook, a top housekeeper and a loving companion. Later on, I resembled my father's side of the family, being raw-boned and fair like he was. He had wide-set grey eyes which marked his Danish roots, he laughed a lot and, like Mum, took each day in its stride.

Mum would on occasions give out a long exasperated sigh and a look would flood her features not unlike a teacher waiting for her students to solve a riddle. She would scratch her head, finger her wedding ring and lean back in her chair when I gave the right answer. She did not need to attend teachers college as she was already an intuitive teacher, yet her eyes were blind to Albert, her only flaw. She never recognised the dragon which lay within.

The dragon must have grown quietly, slowly like the blinking eye of a fish in a boat, sometime between the bashings from his father Alexander. A cankerous sore grew and created a man with an uncontrollable lust which reached out to easy, vulnerable targets. Alexander had acquired a form of snakepit politics. Mum described him as a man who would have an arm draped around his workmates' shoulders. Little did they realise that the draped arm might mean either promotion or destruction; a policy which he used in his advancement. Hands always behind his back and fingers crossed praying to the Devil, she said.

How much of his character was visited upon his son, I often wondered. The final brew of Albert and his evil was bubbling inside, and the genie was let out of the bottle by the time of his teenage years.

*

So, some years after the ritual burning of Elsie's belongings and the removal of any sign of her having ever existed, Albert, who had been a prisoner of war of the Japanese, was shacked up in a caravan at the rear of our house. He was, after all, a revered survivor and a constant reminder of how close we came to being invaded. He too was in denial – of his bag of enticing sexual tricks, which he used to good effect on me, his young half-brother. The chapter which marked my life from then on began.

It started one night when I was sitting on his bed in the caravan. Without warning, he reached over and drew me close into his space. The grip on my body hurt and I grimaced in pain, yet his response was just to whisper, 'Shush.' He eased his grip slightly and smiled exposing his yellow nicotine-stained teeth – those which remained after the others had been knocked out by a rifle butt wielded by a Japanese soldier.

The spittle which dribbled from his lips down his chin, and his staring eyes, blinking like a man walking into sunlight, caused me to look down. His fly buttons were undone and I saw a great purple-headed varmint peering out from his trousers and moving from side to side like a cobra. I broke away and ran out the door.

After breakfast, Albert slithered up alongside me and placed a ten-shilling note in my hand, which I put out of sight. Ten bob was a lot of money then. Another leer formed on his face as he touched his lips in a silent gesture.

I went back each night in spite of my fears and he finally engaged me into massaging his member. Money was handed over at the end of each session and I accumulated twenty pounds within a month and stashed it away My parents never knew and I was not about to tell them, and I had no siblings to talk to.

However, when I talked about it to a kid at school, he said, 'My uncle does the same and gives me money.'

Always in denial, I blocked it out and continued, not understanding the implications of his conduct and my participation. Money ruled my thoughts and I justified it to myself by saying that even if I had told Mum, she just would not have believed it. She was putty in his hands, so I kept the secret.

For his own sneaky reasons, Albert insisted on washing his own sheets and Mum always remarked, 'What a nice independent son, and after everything he endured. And a sad marriage,' she would always add. 'He was too good for Elsie. '

I knew there was no point in ever bringing up the subject. I continued, blocking off thoughts of what I was doing and making money. Besides, my school friend reckoned his uncle was sticking it in his bum by then. From that moment on, I put a hammer in my pocket when I went into his caravan, just in case he touched my bum, and then he would cop it, and hang the consequences.

I played sports – people remarked how fit I looked as I excelled in tennis and swimming – and I and my secret hoard of money both grew.

I knew it would have to stop one day and a plan was forming.

2

Dirk

Dirk had been a Buddhist for as long as he could remember. His kindly parents Dirk and Anna were Buddhists too, and they displayed their empathy to their indigenous charges in the fields on the family farm in the East Indies, sharing the profits with a bonus at the end of each year. There was harmony between Asian and European, and a relationship of mutual respect.

It was a joyous life on the plantation. Dirk had pets of all kind, and a baby elephant which slept with him in the barn at night, Dirk being careful not to let the animal roll over on him. The arrangement had to end, not because of the elephant's bulk but because of the infernal snoring which kept Dirk awake, affecting his daytime studies.

The life they knew and loved came to a violent halt when the Japanese army invaded and inflicted a reign of terror on them. Everyone, including their Asian friends, thought the new overlords would treat them with kindness, but that turned out to be an illusion.

Before the terror, Dirk was employed as a medical orderly in the major hospital in Singapore and he learnt to combine an acceptable mix of formal medicine and holistic cures all of which served him well when he was interned in Changi, along with many Commonwealth soldiers. They were under the command of the brilliant, brave, resourceful 'Weary' Dunlop, who was similar in height to Dirk, well over six feet, which intimidated the small Japanese.

Dirk forced himself to meditate on hatred and how to disperse it because it was not an emotion he had ever allowed to enter into his soul. He struggled with the impulse to hate, particularly once he saw the hatred and contempt the Japanese showed for their charges. He knew he would face a reckoning one day, given his supposed insolence and silence towards them. His height became a focal point, because they had to look up at his face. Invariably he was forced to bow when near them. One of the Aussies said that with his long legs and his head right down he looked like a giant flamingo.

As each day passed in starvation, piles of body waste, blood, death and pain, Dirk's thoughts were of the tap on the neck from the cold steel of the officer's sword and he wondered how painful it would be. There would be lots of blood, he knew, as he had seen some beheadings. It was not a comfortable thought.

Albert Garrison, an Australian medical orderly, was his friend and they shared many tears, many talks and some humour. The Aussies had a wonderful dry wit, with vivid expressions such as 'Ugly as a hatful of arse'oles', 'A head like a robber's dog' and many others. Even in the face of death they would smile and give off some inappropriate remark.

Albert disclosed much of his life to Dirk, describing the hatred between him and his father and how it had affected him. He talked of his sexless marriage to an obsessive Catholic woman, the habitual manual stimulation which he had to resort to in order to quell his uncontrollable lust, and his pre-war trysts with other men in public toilets which left him with a self-loathing, a disgust. What disturbed him most was the fear that his desires might extend to children of tender years. There were times when he spoke of death and told Dirk he would be happy if his life was ended in any fashion, either by his hand or another, such was the fear which he felt closing in on him like a coiled snake.

The Christian religion held no promise and he said, 'A Sunday school teacher and I had a wank together when I was fourteen. Just bloody hypocrites.' And then he went into a fierce dialogue about religion proclaiming, 'The pages of history are littered with the violence perpetuated in the name of Jesus. It's no wonder students of history turn into atheists.'

Dirk had a reply for him. 'The path to God is simple. Just pray, be grateful, try to do good as much as possible.'

'Oh yeah, Dirk. Forgive these rotten little bastards…you've tried. And what about my father? Hatred from the day I was born. Where did that come from?'

Dirk concluded that his advice was not helpful but he was gifted in the art of hypnotism and with the roots of his religion was enshrined a belief in reincarnation. He tried another tactic with Albert concerning his father. Albert agreed to be his subject.

Dirk had no trouble placing him in a trance state. Albert was told to go back to ancient times when he was a young Spartan warrior in 400 BC.

'Tell me your name,' Dirk commanded.

'Arturis.'

'What are you doing?'

'Cleaning my master's shield.'

'Are you going into battle?'

'Tomorrow we fight Darius and his Immortals.'

'How do you feel about your master?'

'I hate him. I hate the way we have sex and he beats me after.' Albert started to shake and sob with sucked-in sighs.

Dirk brought him out the trance.

Albert wiped his eyes and said, 'What did I say?'

Dirk explained homosexual life in Sparta, its cruelty and how some residue had been passed down over the ages, no doubt through other lives, which included his father Alexander.

Albert nodded and was thoughtful.

Dirk ended the session with one more statement. 'Guard against your thoughts straying towards children. It will be your undoing. '

'What do you think I am? A dirty perv?'

Dirk did not reply.

Two weeks later, Dirk knew his ending was close. The tap of the sword had come. He prayed for a quick death, not botched as some. He waved goodbye to all of his friends.

Albert was sad. 'I'll take your place if you like.'

Dirk feared for his friend and what he might become. He pondered on answers to the riddle in Albert's mind.

3

Albert

Albert was born in 1918 in Yorkshire and his father Alexander was forever declariing his hatred of the Scots and how his forebears under Butcher Boy Cumberland put them all – man, woman and child – to the sword after Culloden. Perhaps the hatred deep inside his bodily cells bubbled over and caused him to join the Red Cap Provost Corps in 1914. He was a brutal soldier and told members of the family how he enjoyed shooting deserters.

They immigrated to Australia in the early twenties after the Aussies rejected his army application. Alexander became a prison guard at Yatala in Adelaide and for a time he was the flagellator.

He inflicted a reign of terror on Albert, endlessly beating his son. He tried it once with Blanche, his wife, but she was too strong for him and flung a pot of hot stew in his face; carrots and gravy coursed down his cheeks. On another occasion he tried to hit her and she retaliated by wrenching down the photo of his family in the 1880s which sat over the mantelpiece and chucking it in the fire. He kept his distance from Blanche after that.

Fortune blessed Albert when he was eleven years of age. Alexander was on an invalid pension (which everyone one thought was phoney) and spent all day and night in his own bedroom groaning and crying. Albert knew his misery was about the poor buggers who he had shot in the firing squads and he hoped that their spirits were tormenting his father. Albert believed in God in those days. Alexander had a heart problem and swallowed massive amounts of pills each night.

Blanche was out with her girlfriends when her son heard his father gasping and crying. He went to his father's room and saw that his tablets had spilled and he was reaching for them. Albert whispered a thank you to God and kicked the pills way out of his reach and walked out, closing the door.

His mother came home late and Albert pretended he was asleep on the lounge.

'How's Dad?'

'Asleep.'

She checked him in his room and Albert heard her gasp resounding from the room. He went in rubbing his pretend-sleep eyes and saw the gaping mouth was open and the eyes were fixed and stary.

'Your dad is dead, son.'

'Good '

She smacked his face – the only time she ever did. His life improved from then on but he never told Dirk about what he'd done.

Albert thought about his years of internment and how he had survived. He concluded that it was a miracle which stretched the bow of explanation.

'We have been here for some time,' he scrawled on a piece of paper he had found. 'I don't know how long, because we lost our small stone calendar on the sea voyage to the land of the rising sun. The treasured artefact was thrown overboard along with the sick, the near-dead and the heads which were chopped off. They are merciless – they even beheaded one of their own who refused to carry out an execution.'

They struggled to keep occupied and some just gave up and died. There were no back-breaking tasks like they had in Changi as materials were available. As a consequence, their minds focused continually on food, the how and the why. Religion had gone because they no longer believed in a merciful God.

There was a saying in Changi, 'Home by Christmas or homo by Christmas'. It was not the same in Japan. They needed to conserve every bit of bodily fluid which they could muster. Some had become homosexual in Changi. Albert declined. The thought of kissing a man, or having anal sex or a gobful of prick was never been on his mind. He guessed that when he returned to Australia the old five-finger shuffle would begin again.

Albert always thought he was capable of loving a woman and guessed he was fifty per cent normal. His marriage was and probably still would be a disaster.

His memory wandered back to the honeymoon in 1939 when Elsie came to bed in a neck-to-ankle outfit with her bolting eyes sticking out like a dog's balls and sweat beads across her forehead and clutching her Bible of course. At her throat she wore the huge cross, which she held with both hands inside gloves. 'Maybe the priest had told her not to touch the beastly thing and like a good little Mick she never did,' he muttered

A futile attempt at penetration resulted in her sobbing the Lord's Prayer over and over and he felt like a homeless man outside the huge gates to a mansion pondering on what it would be like to be inside, tucked up nicely, warm and comfortable. He gave up and went outside and jerked off in the garden. The ants enjoyed the surprise feast. It became the template of the sexual married life of Albert Garrison. No children were born as no seed ever entered Elsie's womb, and the thought crossed his mind that Elsie might have longed for a virgin birth. He sought regular release with prostitutes and with other men in public toilets. He never ventured towards children at that point in his life.

Work at the hospital was a blessing. Some like-minded porters joined in a circle to see who could ejaculate first onto a blanket. He stopped when he found out it was his blanket.

Elsie was a good cook, kept an immaculate house and never grumbled, obviously content with the unusual arrangement of their life.

The war changed it all. Medics were needed and he volunteered and sailed away with the 8th Division.

Dirk had kept his friend's emotions under control; he knew he was having an occasional jerk off but never judged him or any of the other men who had turned outright homo. The chats, the excursion into his past life and what it revealed were insightful. Sharing lives with his father explained a lot. Dirk's death only strengthened his hatred towards the Japanese.

There was talk in the camp that a great bomb had exploded on a city and the war might be ending, which might mean they would be executed.

An American plane with its red star encircled flew over: They shot a lot of Japanese and the men cheered as they landed. One of the Yanks was an officer wearing a tie. They rounded up the worst guards, Koreans, and shoved them in an iron cage. A prisoner lit a fire under the cage and the men watched them burn, hollering and screaming. It was too much for the Yanks and one opened fire with his tommy gun and killed them all. Their blood soaked the ground.

They looked at each other and cried and never knew why. Was it freedom or was it the evil they felt within for watching and enjoying the torture of the enemy?

They were fed. And were sick. They drank Coca Cola and smoked Lucky Strikes. But what of the memories and the horror? They slept and dreamed, and all of the horrors spiked their nights.

Albert dreamed he saw Alexander wringing his hands and sitting in a dark cave in the afterlife. Dirk came into the dream and said, 'I felt nothing, just a blow and then I was out and gone towards the light. Go back to God,' he said.

'Perhaps I should heed his advice,' thought Albert, 'but how will I control my sexual side, which will surely arise like a demon from a fiery pit? After all, I'm still young enough with a new stepfather, a great mum and a young half-brother. ' Albert woke from his dream speaking as if Dirk was still in the camp.

4

1955

John

The hot searing winds blew from the west and would twirl around to the north like a dancer in a marathon contest with moments of peak activity, and then without warning a rush was upon us.

I was fifteen years old when my parents, Albert and I traversed the bumpy road to Darwin in a pilgrimage to the place where Dad had served. It seemed like we were driving into a giant sandblaster while Dad was steadfast, holding the two-foot steering wheel, picking along in the converted bus.

He was six years Mum's junior yet it was never a problem or ever remarked on. They worked together at a munitions factory and married in 1939. By 1941 with his engineering skills and road excavation attributes he was stuck in Darwin for some time while I was a baby.

After considerable restoration of the Leyland short-wheelbase bus, the trip was planned with careful eyes and packing of stores. I thought it would have been better to leave my half-brother home to mind the store. However, Mum insisted and with some apprehension I found myself in the rear of the bus with Albert's eyes and hands marking his territory – me – almost like a male lion leaving urine spots around his mate.

I squeezed my legs together and then looked at him with half-opened eyes and lips parted. He was sucked in. I saw the familiar bulge in his trousers. My plan was in its infancy and the first step had been achieved. At fifteen I had had enough of his corruption and wanted no more payment for servicing his needs. My parents were, as usual, blissfully unaware of the body language in the rear of the bus as we rolled along towards some of the spots off the road in the north-west. I had seen the spots in maps and read about the dangers lurking in those areas. A pivotal moment in my life was near and calling.

Dad had a camping spot near a river and placed our camp well back, away from the prowling crocs and the danger signs. I slept under the annex alongside my parents. Albert had his small pup tent some distance away.

Fresh provisions were required and my parents drove off to a property some hours away in order to stock up. I stayed back at the camp with Albert, whose raging lust was obvious. It was dusk and I walked towards the river, treading carefully and passing the danger signs, halting near the river bank. Albert's shuffling feet, which had been damaged by the Japanese, were creeping along behind and I saw his shadow. Flitting. Moving slowly towards me.

He stopped to my left, his favourite side, and on that still night I heard his belt buckle being undone and the flop of his trousers as they touched the twigs on the bank. There was a full moon and I wondered if the man in the moon was looking at us both. When Albert handed me a five-pound note, I quickly thrust it into my pocket.

I placed my left hand on his back and grabbed his member with my right, gently inching him towards the bank. His eyes were closed while the usual performance was carried out. I heard the splash of a large crocodile as it moved semi-submerged towards us.

At the moment when he began to moan in his pleasure, I shoved him with my hand and he plunged into the river. His eyes were wide in an expression of sadness just when the large croc took him across the head and shoulders, snapping its jaws. I heard a stifled scream and Albert disappeared from sight. Apart from some splashing, with the water being churned into mud, the scene became quiet.

I walked back to the camp feeling in my pocket. The five-pound note was still there but Albert had gone. I shook for a while when the reality of what I'd done came into focus, but Mum and Dad arrived soon after. They asked me where Albert was.

'Dunno. Went for a walk, I think.'

I heard them thrashing around in the scrub, and Mum calling out.

'Bit dangerous in the dark. Let's look in the daylight,' Dad muttered.

We drove off to the station and finally the local police arrived. A grey-haired cop took Mum out of earshot and spoke to her. I heard her gasp and she was wringing her hands and scratching the top of her head, as she did when she was worried.

A fruitless search was conducted and all that was found was a pair of torn and stained khaki trousers.

We turned round and drove back to Adelaide. Mum cried all the way. Dad was silent.

Huge crowds attended Albert's service. Australia had lost one of its stoic heroes.

I had a different view and by now my dissonance was deeply imbedded, locked in place by my denial. But my money stash was looking good.

Albert

The searing pain after the first bite was silenced by the mud which flooded his mouth and caused his heart and lungs to stop. Albert felt a whooshing inside his torn body and looked back. He saw his young brother walking away and in that moment he knew he had passed out of his human life, a fact which became obvious when old comrades and relatives walked towards him. They took his hand and he smelt a familiar mushroom smell which filled his nostrils on his new journey. He knew it was the odour of his first nocturnal emission. Elsie came alongside him and smiled with a radiant vision which flooded her features. A sinking feeling came upon him in that instant and it was as if he was shedding a skin. In those split seconds, a brighter world of colours which were outside the spectrum heralded an episodic panorama of his life: the unfolded dramas were each encased inside encapsulated moments.

He imagined he would wave goodbye to all of his earthly friends, but the program of life went into fast forward. The letter which he intended to write to young John about the evil he had inflicted became stalled, along with his denial, which had been given another chance to survive.

He could smell Elsie's cooking when the odours of garlic mixed with tomatoes permeated the house. How he wished that his dreams had come to fruition – of how she might mould into his arms so that they would be folded together, like two spoons in a cutlery drawer. He looked at Elsie and knew she saw his dream because she smiled again without any of the resentment she might have had about the years of non-communication when his married life was in a shambles and he was powerless to fix it. The only joy she had given him was in the clean clothes she provided. Had he taken her – the clothes and the food – for granted?

Once her illness settled in and she began the race towards oblivion, her covert consumption of brandy became overt – he heard the sounds of her slurping at the rear of the house. On checking later, he saw the empty bottles littered about in the long grass, which he had not mown. She became decadent, smelling sour, her eyes bloodshot and her face mottled. Occasionally her breath would return to normal after noisily gargling large quantities of lavender water. Yet the smokey smell of the brandy seemed to flood her body cells, seeping out beyond what aura she had. She would open her mouth in an effort to conceal the odour. It reminded him of the prostitutes he once sought and the gargling sound they made when they guzzled their favourite spirit to lessen the taste of the residue of sexual fluids. In an act of rare empathy, he had provided his poor afflicted wife from then on with a weekly supply of good bottled brandy, no doubt hastening her untimely end.

Sadness enveloped him, circling like a mosquito in a bedroom, unable to be caught, buzzing and landing, searching for weak spots on the flesh from which blood would be drawn.

Albert's vision changed to Changi and Dirk, and the comedy they had shared, until the veil lifted and showed the misery on the other side. Dirk draped his arm around his friend and guided him towards a grotto, a dark cave with misty tendrils of slimy undergrowth. He stepped across the muddy water on stepping stones with faces of Japanese soldiers engraved upon the surface and he heard their groans when he trod on each stone. There were no words spoken by Dirk, yet Albert knew when he entered the dark cave and sat on a mossy rock that he was to be still, and silent, leaving only when he had contemplated his life.

5

Blanche

There was an unbridled wrath floating somewhere in their mother's cells which inexorably affected the two sisters, Rose and Blanche. They did not confide in their wounded old Boer War veteran father Harold, who hobbled about like a cockroach with arthritis. He was banished by the unreasonable matriarch of the family to the toilet, where he spent many hours smoking his old pipe and the Navy ready-rubbed fine-cut tobacco which he was fond of.

The sisters surmised that their mother might have been unjustly treated in some distant past life, its echoes lingering, awaiting a possible form of propitiation which would soften or soothe her hostility and satisfy her need for vengeance.

Blanche subconsciously blocked out most of her tender years because of her mother's raging high-pitched voice screeching on top note, coupled with a plethora of thrown pots and pans, threats with knives and forks, and uneaten dinners chucked on the floor, all ending with some quote from the Bible. Her mother was at her worst when the soup ladles were bounced around the kitchen. Her foaming lips sprayed spittle and her bolting eyes spewed venom at anyone within her space, her Adam's apple bobbing up and down all the while, like a stationary steam engine.

Rose and Blanche developed courage in their mid-teens and started chucking back the soup ladles, the pots, the pans, the forks and the knives. Rose scored a hit with the cast-iron frying pan, which knocked their mother to the ground. She brushed them off when they tried to pick her up, instead yelling out to Harold in the yard, 'Get in here.' He came in and sat her on a chair and under her guidance began to sew up the gaping wound. There was no way she would go to a doctor, because it might prompt questions about why her daughters had struck back. They watched while the needle was stuck and pulled tight. Not a sound came from her lips, though they quivered slightly. But her eyes were narrowed and glittering with all the spite which she could muster: the hate circled around in the room and Rose took a knife to bed with her for the next two weeks.

In between her bouts of hatred, she spent many hours singing in the choir, where she was Queen of the May, at the Methodist Church. Those sanctimonious folk considered her to be a saint and used that handle for her to all who would listen about her qualities, her knowledge of the scriptures, yet they were not aware of her surreptitious sucking on her favourite bottle of Scotch.

To her credit she taught her daughters to cook, sew, knit, iron and keep a good house and garden. Of course the teaching was always accompanied by a cane across the fingers.

Blanche never knew a time when her mother said, 'I love you.' She was in tears after a session and yelled out, 'Do you love me?' which was greeted with her right ear being nearly yanked off. Blanche gave up on any form of communication with her from that moment on.

Blanche was sixteen when she gave birth to Albert in 1918. It was a sort of payback to the old tyrant, as she said in later years. Harold said nothing as usual but his wife raged for days, finally muttering about what the church would say. The father and soon-to-be husband, Alexander Garrison, was an army policeman who looked good in his red hat and uniform. He came home on leave and that is when it happened. Not long after he had hung his cue in the rack, Blanche was pregnant.

The sisters moved out and boarded with a charming Catholic couple (which put the mockers on any further relationship with their mother). Rose's situation improved when she married in early 1918 before the bubble in the belly became blatantly obvious. Their mother never attended the wedding, which suited the girls. They never saw her again and did not wish to. However, Rose felt sorry for her dad, believing that her letters would have been intercepted.

Rose became a nurse in France towards the close of the war and nursed back to health a Canadian soldier who was a victim of mustard gas. They fell in love and married, and she returned to Canada with him.

Alexander and Blanche moved to Australia after the war and made a fresh start in Blair Athol. Their mother was left to shrivel and die, a lonely old woman, in an insane asylum. Rose was told of it after a virulent letter arrived from the choir espousing her cause and blasting the girls for their lack of empathy. Harold had moved to an old soldiers' home and Rose visited him before he died. It caused her some tears, yet she recovered; after all, he should have stood up against the vile woman. And they were her last words on the subject of her mother.

The warm weather in Australia was pleasant and Alexander found employment as a prison guard, which would have suited him as he had some sadistic tendencies born of a distorted view of life. They were lucky to be in receipt of wages, as the depression was looming.

Alexander had many social problems and for some reason was brutal to their son all of his life. Blanche intervened on many occasions and Alexander became quiet when she threatened him. Along with heart problems, a form of early dementia engulfed him and he was put out on a pension. The problems took his life in 1929. Blanche did not grieve unduly as he had been a morose man yet he had given her a son and an escape to another country.

Albert grew and found employment as a porter in a hospital. He met and married Elsie, prissy Elsie, of whom Blanche did not approve.

Another war came along. Blanche had been working in a munitions factory alongside Edward Taylor. He was six years younger but they enjoyed each other's company and married in 1939. To her surprise, she became pregnant with John, who was born in 1940.

Albert was in the army by then and with the 8th Division later on.

He was captured by the Japanese and held in Changi. His marriage was in tatters before he left and they received very few letters.

After the bombing, Edward served in Darwin as an engineer and he was also away for long periods. Blanche's life was, however, busy with her child and volunteer work and she kept herself busy in the garden as much as she could.

Life rolled on. John was growing, the war was over. Elsie died of cancer and Albert came to live with his mother in a van. Tragically he was taken by a crocodile while they were on a camping trip to Darwin. His body was never recovered. Blanche was offered a trip back to Yorkshire but declined. 'The country of my birth holds nothing but bitter memories. Australia is my home and I'll die here,' she told the RSL.

6

John

I review my life at the beginning of each new year. I find it cleans out any demons and preserves my sanity. The review involves some resolutions and exploration of my past, present and future journey into the unknown and questions about how my personality was shaped. It sounds pompous, but detractors seem to forget we are required to adopt an exacting approach when conducting our affairs.

To be where I am now from the time when I was corrupted by Albert is a quantum leap which still amazes me. I am amazed with my success and the trappings which accompany my good fortune. My wife Penelope is the apogee, a part of my plan, whereby I moved to a leafy affluent suburb and practised my ballroom dancing and sharply hone my tennis skills.

My intuition had been on high alert as I scouted around for a wealthy prospect. The res gestae in legal terms was the ingredient, the catalyst which propelled my antennae towards the wealthy daughter of former landowners.

I truly loved and still do love the pretty Penelope. She has been the bonus in my life. Within a few months of wooing her, I proposed marriage and she accepted. I joined the Church of England where her parents worshipped and we were married there. The matter of God and religion had long disappeared from my focus, but I was able to mutter and mumble the prayers along with the rest of the congregation. I look to myself for my own valediction in all matters.

Her parents paid for our honeymoon in Paris, where I was on my best behaviour. Our wedding gift, a large house in the leafy suburb of Hawthorn, was waiting for us when we returned.

Yet the black cloud of deviant sexual antics hovered and drove my body to ache, stabbing at my senses over the years. As partners I chose men like me, never getting embroiled except for a quick release. I had too much to lose if I were to be discovered in an illicit sex act.

*

I guess most lives are a series of chapters and mine is no different, except for my secret illegal acts of so many years ago. There were major changes after I entered university as a law student.

My parents Edward and Blanche were not in desperate straits, as Dad worked as a supervisor at the General Motors Holden plant at Woodville and Mum worked in the canteen. They sold the Blair Athol house and moved to a bigger block at Medindie Gardens and I boarded with them during my time at the university. My secret stash was mounting and I topped it up with part-time work in many jobs.

Their faces were beaming at my graduation.

Mum said, 'I wish Albert could see this.'

I nodded and when they walked away I hummed, 'Never smile at a crocodile.'

Mum died in 1987, crying her eyes out and calling out 'Albert' from her nursing home bed.

Dad died shortly after; he missed his beloved Blanche. Penelope and Jacki loved them both. Jacki had returned from overseas for a short time.

My parents' house was left to Jacki. She later sold it. Penelope visits Jacki in Switzerland, where she lives with her engineer, and they do not intend to live in Australia. My in-laws died around the same time as Mum and Dad. My wife holds the title to our house; her father insisted on it. Being a lawyer, I organised it. Silly me, because in reality all I have is the business. I must be careful with my secrets.

I don't know who the ringmaster is who controls my inner thoughts. Perhaps he is a sadist, because he has developed a style which has me darting between major events like Christmas, Albert, driver's licence, job, marriage, a child and my lies.

*

I never looked back after I found employment with a well known law firm. I had had a stint as a junior in a firm which specialised in criminal law, but I knew my future was in civil law.

I remember my interview for the position. I had coached myself for weeks. I had not a shred of remorse over the death of Albert and that fact remained as a constant for the majority of my life.

The interview with the senior partners was lengthy and many probing questions were asked. I needed to prepare myself and I took some time to sandpaper some of my edges, evening out the rough spots in order to provide a smooth surface which a panel would be comfortable with, so that any awkward questions could easily slide past without much effort. I felt like a man who had fallen in a sandblaster and came out shiny and carbolicly scrubbed.

'Your preparation is almost perfect, John,' one member said.

An air of anticipation hung in the atmosphere like a humid night before the wet season and settled in. A protracted silence followed as if they had a question hanging in the air, like 'Is he for real?'

One of the panel broke the silence, pursuing my admission that two weeks ago I had not been sure how I would give my answers. 'How are you different now?'

'A lot less edgy,' I replied

The process concluded and I left the room with a confident upright stance.

The Senior Partners

The partners looked at one another.

'What do you reckon, Fred?'

'A clever man. Almost like he studied our minds.'

'Hmm.'

'Is he just a bit too clever? Perhaps a ruthless streak?'

Jack spoke. 'Something tells me we should employ him, although are we providing him with a career which might end in sadness?'

'Dunno. He's the best so far, but I agree there is something intangible about him, like a machine without a soul. A man of some secrets, I suspect.'

The three men signed off on John's appointment. Little did they realise how accurate their predictions would be.

7

John

It is 1 January and I wonder if my life has just been an illusion, leading to another illusion, the consequences of which will slap my face like the bended branch of a tree. Those slaps seem to be more frequent as I lurch towards an early old age.

How does personality evolve? Is it a symphony of people, of parents, friends, workmates and of course genes? I don't like to think about genes, as that is too close to Albert. Personality ought to be built like a house, with pieces coming together from the foundations. However, that conglomeration of situations is not originally created by us. They are just happenings and, like emotions, should pass on.

The question remains: who are we? Maybe we are like actors mouthing the lines – getting them right, yet forgetting the hidden music behind the lines. Telling the story, but not showing it.

I have one of those disaster dreams, wherein my ringmaster, the choreographer of my tap dance, lets me down and Penelope, as the secret understudy, will rise from her secondary position and assume command. And then I will be undone.

*

I had a close call a few years ago when the madness, the impulsive acts and the uncontrolled thoughts returned to haunt my soul. We were on a vacation in Bangkok and after two hours of endless shopping (one of my pet aversions) with Pen, I made my escape and met up with a couple of friends, Tom and Ray, who I had contacted before our departure. They were Vietnam veterans who were both afflicted with arthritis and broken marriages; they had found that the Thai climate suited them. We had crossed paths years ago when I used them as investigators, gathering evidence in false claims.

I walked to the address they had given me and was warmly greeted by both men with much back slapping and chuckles. They poured drinks and chit chat floated in the air. Then the flippant remarks came to a halt and serious looks appeared on their faces,. I sat forward in anticipation of what was to come .

They produced photos of very young children involved in sex acts and I took a breath as I viewed each of the horrors. Tom placed a report on the coffee table. Inside were the identity cards of my two friends, and Thai police warrant cards. They explained they were shadowing Australian paedophiles and gathering evidence. One of the suspects was a young man who I had a tryst with years ago. I read the attached report.

The suspect said, 'I went to my lawyer's office, a bloke called John Taylor, who was my sexual partner for a while. He wasn't there – he's not a paedophile – but I trust him.'

I could not look at my friends.

Ray spoke first, 'We're not judging you at all, John. We're gay ourselves – you didn't know, did you?'

I just shook my head and remained mute, my thoughts contemplating disaster.

Tom spoke. 'This bloke is full on. If he contacts you, I suggest you don't appear for him, OK? He'll do bulk time over here. Let him rot.'

'OK, I got the message.'

'Let's have a drink for old times, what do you say?'

I replied between slurs, 'Love Pen but, shit, what if she found out?'

'Yeah, mate, we know. Just distance yourself.'

I nodded and gulped down the grog.

I returned to our hotel room to be greeted by a sharp Penelope, her eyes flaring.

'Where the bloody hell have you been?'

'Met up with Tom and Ray - used to work for us,' and I lied about the rest. I could not wait to get out of the place.

I think a sign was sent to me on that day. I hoped my past would not rise again, spewing green bile like the exorcist girl with her head turning round 360 degrees.

*

Len was a junior partner in the firm and within the space of weeks we had become involved. It lasted until he was killed in a car crash. I missed him. However, I determined to lie low for a time to concentrate on being a good husband and father to our beloved only child Jacki.

I have not had any so-called affairs for years. Mind you, the shadow manifests when the vision of Len appears. However, I just turn over and go to sleep. The love I feel for Pen has deepened in a funny sort of way which is indescribable: I know the twin forces of good and evil are lying low in their little crucible.

What is evil anyway? Are we born with it or is it the strongest form of possession, sitting like an onion with layers awaiting their removal. Has my ego created an inner monster? Or have I just been gliding through life without being touched or moved by anything?

And what is happiness? Really only harmony and contentment, I reckon. Perhaps life's goals are just to be vital and consistent in all aspects, which my mother felt was the way to go; she lost herself in music, the garden and insightful books which created a spiritual life. Her Nirvana was a few steps away all the time I knew her.

My life has been punctuated with illusion on top of illusion, interlaced with brief encounters which supposedly create my happiness.

The last encounter made me feel sick. I have been inexorably following my demon on a relentless journey.

Jacki

Jacki believed there was something missing within her father, though she loved him dearly She never mentioned it to her mum, who adored her life, her marriage and her faith in God and his grace. Jacki had a gut feeling at times when she thought their marriage would end in a screaming shouting match. She knew she had a privileged life. 'I must have done something very good in a past life to have such luxury in this one, living in Switzerland with a great man and lover,' she concluded.

There is a downside for most people and hers was an inability to bear children. However, she would whisper, reminding herself, 'I think about what I have, my health and all the trimmings and I soon forget the bad things. Frederick loves my parents and I his.'

However, Frederick once said something that still stuck like fly paper. 'Does John ever speak about his early life as a kid?'

'No. Why?'

There was a pause. (There were usually pauses when Frederick pondered an answer.)

'You've met my uncle – the detective, Uncle Al – you know?'

I nodded.

'He's on a child sex task force.'

Jacki was impatient. 'Get to the point, Fred.'

'He was sexually abused as a kid by an older uncle. His persona and the way he speaks and looks are just like your dad.'

She was silent and thoughtful yet a fire had been lit within her which would only be extinguished when she found the truth

8

Penelope

Penelope always brought home stray dogs. 'Maybe it's the need within me to mother,' she would say to herself, 'something which my parents excelled in.' She missed them both since their untimely passing.

'A life of debauchery and its trappings holds no promise for me,' she told her friends, though personal vanity did allow her to indulge in facials and botox; along with good food, good wine and the gym. She did not smoke. Her style may have developed very early in her excellent life and, regardless of the wealth (which was to be used wisely, as her dad pronounced without fail each Sunday after church), she had an abiding empathy for people who had fallen on hard times or just slipped through the cracks. She found an outlet for her empathy by being a social worker in a government agency and by making generous donations to charities.

That is a broad-brush picture of Penelope Taylor (whose friends called her Pen). She was married to a man with an ability to scheme and with a ruthless streak running through his veins. Where it came from she had no idea because her in-laws were wonderful people. Perhaps it was because of his achievements in life and his profession. 'Having to carefully dissect facts and turn them into intelligence is the key,' she assured herself.

Pen had fallen in love with John when she met him some thirty years ago. He had the golden look of a Norseman, she told her daughter, and I still don't know of his roots. John was slightly under six feet with the lean hard build of an Iron Man contestant, the long-legged, raw-boned, smooth-muscle type. Not overlarge but in proportion, she thought, and he had always been endowed with good health, his parents told her. What body hair he had was golden and curly. He had a light facial tan over an equally light olive skin.

She liked his eyes and noted they were the palest of blue while hers were hazel. Jacki had inherited the amazing aquamarine eyes. He reminded Pen of those Prussian German soldiers in the SS with the looks of an angel mixed with a demon. Not that he was a demon – though he can be in bed at times, she smirked to herself; he just turned out to be a secretive man. Her dad had felt uncomfortable about him – he was never able to nail John down, and said so – and had insisted on a prenuptial agreement.

Outwardly, John developed some empathy for the folk under her control and he never once queried the amount of cash which she donated to charity. However, she suspected that it was a charade and once wondered if he was an alien – one of those walk-ins who are written about in New Age books.

She discussed the positives of her marriage with her friend Shirley. 'I'm married to a well presented man with good parentage who never seems to put a foot wrong, appears to love our life and never grumbles, yet his mind always seems to be in overdrive.'

Shirley nodded.

Pen noted that he loved their daughter and their friends yet never spoke about his life as a kid and the half-brother who had been a prisoner of war and lived with them after the war. 'It's as though Albert never existed.'

Shirley nodded once again.

Penelope was a virgin when they married and there never seemed to be any difficulties with sex during their marriage. There was a problem earlier on when she queried him about his going to sleep without any conversation after the act. She gave up after some nagging and reading about it in a book. She came to the conclusion that he may have felt some abandonment in his life.

She questioned him once. 'Why, John? Why?'

'Be happy with us, Pen. Be happy.'

And that was the only response she ever got from him.

They had a good array of friends. Some of the single mums tried to make out with John and were treated with silent stony stares, so that part of their marriage was on solid ground. Added to that he was attentive at times, a mild drinker and a great swimmer and tennis player.

She put any pinpricks of doubt about the marriage out of her mind, yet concluded she was in denial for a time.

The pinpricks returned after an unexpected conversation with the widow of his former partner Len. Len was killed in a car crash and it upset John, as it would. They offered financial help to his young wife Linda and their baby by giving them a small mortgage on a unit they owned.

Years later she saw Linda at a market and stopped for a chat. Linda had remarried and her new pregnancy was coming along fine. Her husband Bill was a policeman.

Penelope was shocked by what she heard.

'Len was a bisexual and he moved around public toilets. Bill was a vice cop back then and remembers taking Len's name after a complaint.'

'What, the handsome Len?'

'Yep. I didn't know at the time, but I found out later. I confronted him when another cop knocked on our door.'

'What did he do?'

'Drove off in a rage, pissed and hit a tree. You know the rest.'

'Did Bill confirm all this after you met?'

'Yes. Before Bill I was getting phone calls from strange men who would hang up when they heard my voice.'

'Shit,' Penelope said.

'His sister told me later that her brother was bi.'

They parted company and Penelope never saw Linda again. However, the seeds of alarm now began to grow at a startling rate.

*

The seeds sprouted wings. Penelope dreamed of a butterfly which flitted near her ear and said, 'Wake up. Wake up.'

The combination of all she knew from Linda, her husband and Jacki (and what Frederick had said) seemed to corroborate her suspicions. She came to believe that John had had a succession of affairs with other men. She hatched a plan which she hoped would reveal the truth. The plan would not be a full-on confrontation or require the services of a private investigator. It would be just a subtle form of entrapment. She brooded on her plan and was satisfied the bait would work.

She knew John's radar was finely tuned; his ears were up like a hyena on the scent. If the slightest hint of suspicion entered his mind, it would spoil the plan. If her intuition proved right and it worked, she would have to be strong enough to end the marriage, which was a hard thing to contemplate.

She had a card made up with an enticing promise which could be assessed as a sexual advertisement. Friends would be waiting in hiding, without any knowledge of the underlying reason for the surprise 'birthday party'. A day, a date and a time and place were added. If John came to the party, then her question would be answered.

9

John

I never knew Mum's first husband yet I spied two photos of him in the old battered soap box: one showed a man in a British Army Provost Corps uniform with the red cap adorning his small head; the other showed him in a high-collared blue, buttoned-up affair with tunic pockets as worn by prison warders in Australia. And in both photos he looked very grim, with his hats worn right down, almost covering his eyes, as was the fashion back then.

No one who was still around from those days spoke about him. Albert was about eleven when his father died and I heard snippets in the air that our mother was lonely for a short time. However, she was a survivor, a great cook, an equally top gardener, a charitable woman.

It's easy to imagine what a catch Mum would have been to Edward: almost like Carter when he found the Valley of the Kings. The prying eyes and the surreptitious moving back of curtains, as was the fashion then, when people spied on their neighbours and marked calendars, would have ensured a short wooing period. They married in 1939 and to her surprise I was born in 1940, a year after the tongues stopped wagging.

I heard about the well loved Albert on so many occasions. Photos were constantly flashed before my eyes and every night Mum walked around in circles with the shell-framed photo, her knuckles white from her tight grip on the frame, muttering to God incessantly. 'Bring him home safe, bring him home safe, please God.'

Dad would be in bed by then, probably pretending to be asleep. I was lulled into sleep by the chanting.

After the war ended, Albert came home to a hero's welcome, inside and outside the house. Most of the hugs, tears and laughs were reserved for Mum. Oh, I got a pat on the head and a Japanese helmet. Elsie was there holding her cross but she didn't seem to get a look in. Elsie was different; she was the woman who ruined Albert's life. Years after the passing of the poor woman, Mum could be heard to say, 'She's not mourned. She's probably better off in the afterlife.'

Within a few weeks, Albert had erected a tent in his backyard, where his wife served his meals. Other prisoners of war behaved in similar ways.

Dad remarked on the odd arrangement. 'Poor buggers. Maybe they feel trapped in the house.'

Did Mum ever have a mild suspicion about Albert, I wondered, but Albert was so cunning, so devious in his body language that he was able to mask it. Mum would never have believed her favourite son would have sunk so low.

His fitful sleep was laced with screams so loud that they could be heard from our place. No doubt his visions of horror must have also included sexual encounters with other males which he must surely have had before he left to join the army.

Albert would never attend a theatre or listen to a war tune, like a Noel Coward song, or read about the Nazi concentration camps, because it would invoke a tirade about the fat bums that sat on chairs, the women who ran off with the Yanks and the hated Japanese who should have been wiped off the face of the earth. Once a year, drunken relief after the Anzac Day march would soften his restless soul until the nasties reared again. He would remain half sloshed for the week after Anzac Day and his employers at the Royal Adelaide Hospital would ignore his absence.

He was, after all, one of our heroes. That was my mother's signature tune.

*

When I matured, I recognised I had been denying that I had actually been prostituting myself. My heart yelled to me in dreams, 'It must stop.' But the enticing talons of money gripped my higher thoughts.

I recalled Mum's philosophy and her profound wisdom expressed in the sayings which tumbled out on occasions. Sayings such as 'We must accept the uncertainty of life and what it brings. Express gratitude for the twists and the turns and the beauty which lies beneath when the veil is lifted.' And another was 'We should not take ourselves too seriously, to ride above the waves of emotion.' And 'The human way is to put ourselves first. The spiritual way is to understand other people's feelings and to know that we are all imperfect.'

She read many books, the Scriptures in particular. I still have her Bible, though I haven't opened it for some time. When I reflect on my life, I think I should have followed in her footsteps.

I ask myself how I have managed to justify my strange life and conceal for so long its secrets – Albert's death and my dual sexuality. Yet here I am, a well respected member of the community. Maybe the detachment I learned in my legal career has enabled my dissonance to thrive and prosper.

The term paedophile was unknown to society in those days. Instead they were called 'dirty old men'. Most were in gaol. Being a person who encountered child abuse, I have read a great deal on the topic in my legal career. Much of the material tells of the curse which affects families in future generations – 'visited upon the sons', as the Bible accurately says.

I know I am not a paedophile, and I have never had the desire to inflict pain on children. However, there were opportunities in my law practice to appear for some defendants. I never did.

*

Then came the pivotal moment which unfolded as a result of my momentary lapse of attention – that moment when Pen discovered my other life and arranged the surprise birthday party. I was sucked into the trap like a fly drawn to an insect-devouring plant; there was no return.

A huge gulf opened between us which made it impossible to find a point of agreement. We parted and that was that. She went off to Switzerland to stay with Jacki and I was left in the rumpus room to ponder my future.

My life has become a black desert with no rest. I recall the scars with a haunting vision of doom when I hear a jingle, a lonely love song or even a piano being played drunkenly in a movie. I watched *Casablanca* on the Hallmark Channel, and that caused an enormous flood of tears which came and went in fits and starts all night long. Albert's sad eyes stared above my head for a split second.

When I looked in the bathroom mirror the next morning, I turned away from what I saw – a face holding an expression saying, 'What have I done?'

I had to find a way, a way back through the maze in which I was lost. It came when I went for a walk and asked for my mother to help me. It sounds stupid, I know, but on my return I called into a health shop to purchase some almonds. I was surfing the shelves when staring at me was a packet of blanched almonds. Blanched. Blanche… that's it, that's it…she had spoken. I walked out munching the nuts and saw an open church (one of those alternative ones that are dotted around). I read a sign which was being posted up at that moment: 'Blanche Street.' I staggered and nearly fell; my heart raced.

The pastor ran towards me. 'Are you OK?' His face was a mirror of my father's.

I smiled back after a deep breath and said, 'I'm all right now. All right now. I see it all.' And I walked away smiling to myself.

I prayed to God that night and asked him to forgive my apostasy. There was a strange blue light in the room. Mum's Bible lay open on the floor. It must have fallen off the bed during the night. The pages of the book flicked open and I lit on a passage: Matthew 6: 5–6. I read it out loud as the blue light faded: 'And whenever you pray, do not be like the hypocrites; for they love to stand and pray in the synagogue and at street corners so that they may be seen by others. Truly I tell you they have received their reward. But whenever you pray go into your room and shut the door and pray to your father in secret. And your father who sees you in secret will reward you.'

The epiphany which I experienced stirred within me a need to speak about it. I rang my office and informed them I was taking three months off, which caused some surprise as I never had time off work. I typed out a statement telling as much as I could remember and then rang a retired detective who I saw on occasions. Dave was a school chum and also a Freemason. We agreed to meet soon. I scrawled in my diary, 'NO MORE DENIAL.'

We had a chat about small stuff – the usual: weather, politics – and then Dave spoke.

'How can I help you, John?'

I thrust the statement at him.

He read it very carefully, his lips moving as he silently mouthed the words of the text. Then he spoke. 'So you say you pushed Albert into a river and crocs killed him?'

'Yes.'

'Any witnesses?'

'No.'

'And it was the end product of his abuse?'

'Yes.'

Dave paused, then spoke, carefully enunciating each word. 'Had you fallen asleep before?'

'Yes.'

'Did you dream of Albert?'

'Always.'

'How do you know that you didn't dream what happened?'

I did not answer.

'Look, you were fifteen years old, he corrupted you for years, you planned his death and he died. Right?'

I nodded.

'How can you be sure after all these years that the story is real?'

I stammered, 'Well, I…'

'Sorry, John. It could have been a dream He may have walked to the edge and been taken in by a croc on the bank. Don't you see?'

I shook my head.

Dave handed me a card with the name of a hypnotist and added, 'We used this guy a lot. He'll get to the bottom of it. Many people confess to things which they only dreamed they did.'

There was a long pause.

Then Dave concluded. 'See this bloke before you do anything foolish. Promise me?'

I nodded. 'I promise, Dave. For sure.'

We shook hands and walked away.

*

I booked a fishing trip to Ceduna on the west coast and was to fly there in a few days. However, I sent an email to my loved ones in Switzerland. I added an attachment which included everything I had said to Dave and mentioned the appointment with the hypnotist in five weeks' time. I spoke about my secret life and how it had come about and my epiphany and how I had found God, and I wrote about my coming trip to Ceduna. I was unsure whether Pen would answer. I dared not mention a possible reconciliation.

Now I'm about to drive to the airport for my flight.

10

Denial Bay is in the Ceduna area of the west coast. Once known as Mackenzie, the small township was the site of the earliest settlement in the region during colonial days. Matthew Flinders explored the coast and from the sea, through his telescope, he was of the opinion that the bay would be a good place to start exploration inland. Journeys found him to be wrong. The name Denial Bay stuck.

John boarded the charter for a good day's fishing. The area to which they were headed was well known for many fish and great white sharks. It was a cloudy day yet the sea was calm as they ploughed deep into the ocean, searching with the help of the fish finder. The crew and three others were on board and bait was caught on the way out.

John snagged his leg on a hook but the hook was removed and a Band-Aid was applied.

In spite of many changes in location, the fishing had been good. Now the winds had blown in and the sea was choppy.

The skipper looked towards the horizon and saw what appeared to be a white sail flapping on the water, a sign of an overturned yacht. The skipper said to himself, 'Bloody fools to be out this far.' He steered towards the sail and when the boat was about thirty metres away he saw the figure of a small boy, about ten years old, clinging to the side of the overturned vessel. He advised the coastguard of the location, and moved slowly towards the yacht.

They were within ten metres and closing when John made an impulsive decision. The child was in distress and sinking. John grabbed a length of rope and dived in, swimming fast towards the boy, who had sunk. John dived in and found him, pushing him to the surface. The child was breathing. John made a loop on the rope with his left hand, at the same time slinging the rope across the boy's back and around his chest. Remembering the ultimate non-slip knot from his Boy Scout days, he then tied a bowline by bringing the short end up through the loop and over the top and bringing it down again through the loop. He rolled the boy on his back and ensured that the rope was tight around his chest before signalling to the crew to tow him in, which they did. The crew were able to haul him in, as the distance between the boats had shrunk to four metres.

John was about to clamber back into the boat when he felt a heavy nudge on his leg where the Band-Aid had been applied. He was bumped again and felt a terrific pain in his lower body.

A giant white shark shot out of the water with John encased in its mouth. The men watched in silent horror as both man and shark sank below the surface. The last remaining sign of John was blood and bubbles.

They turned around after a short time and headed back, their faces forlorn and the boy wrapped in a blanket, alive because of the heroism of John Taylor.

A search was conducted but no sign of John or the parents of the boy was ever found.

Penelope

Penelope read the email John had sent. It answered many questions and she was prepared to start again, mainly because of his new faith in God. She thought there was a chance for them. Jacki wanted it also and they both pondered on it. Then the letter arrived from a friend with the newspaper cutting describing the heroism which had caused John's death. It left Penelope in distraught and in shock.

Nothing could bring John back, so it was just a matter of returning to her home and preparing for a commemoration service. John was to be honoured with a bravery medal. Jacki and Frederick came along to assist in the grieving.

The medal was awarded at Government House six months later

and Penelope was at home afterwards, with Jacki. She took out the email with its attachment and placed it on a plate in the microwave and watched it shrivel into blue flame then ashes, symbolising that these were his last words to his family. They would remain as cryptic ashes. There was to be no more residue from Albert's death and John's name would be enshrined along with all the other heroes of history.

Dave was there when the deed was done and said in a sad voice, 'So it goes.'

Jacki remarked, 'He was my dad and my hero and nothing will change that.'

After reading his diary, everyone joined hands and chanted a mantra, 'No more denial.'

Epilogue

Jacki and Frederick returned to their Swiss home; they occasionally visit Penelope and she makes return trips.

In spite of the urgings from her daughter and her son-in-law, Penelope has no intention of living outside Australia. She has her gym, her bushwalking and, of late, watercolour painting. These are combined with her charity work. She has retired from her job and has employed a live-in housekeeper/manager because the house is now full of exchange students who all need to be fed. Sea voyages, on which she is usually accompanied by her daughter, are a joy to her. She has blocked any painful memories of John's betrayal by attending therapy classes.

Yet there are some nights – particularly humid still nights when the atmosphere is heavy, full of static electricity – when a lingering scent of his Old Spice dances around. It is then that she feels the presence of his spirit. And remembers the life they had.

Shaken & Stirred

'If you ever wake up without a problem, you had better get down on your knees and pray, because you just died.'
Norman Vincent Peel

Prologue

Bob Allen's Third Court Appearance

The missus and me have been packed in this courtroom like sardines for two hours. Not one person has been called up. They couldn't because the beak isn't here yet and it's now ten forty-five a.m. and I keep reading the summons, which clearly says ten a.m. I've got to get out of here and listen to the bad news from the quack. Meanwhile, my poor missus has to explain to the beak why I'm not here. Why can't these legal generals be on time like the rest of us common herd? Bloody ignorant bastards.

Twelve-thirty p.m. It's bad news…the cancer has grown and I have to explain to the beak why I wasn't here.

He removes his glasses and stares at me, silent for a few seconds – maybe to scare me but it doesn't work. 'So you say you had a medical appointment?'

'Yep,' I says without any 'sir' added. Why he asked that I don't know because Mavis had already told him, and handed in a copy of the visit times just after I left, when he'd reluctantly decided to come into his courtroom.

'I am considering rescinding your bail, Mr Allen.'

My temper flared right then. I looked him in the eye and said, 'Go for it, cockhead.'

He leaned back in his chair sucking on his glasses and looked at the sheriff officer (who had by now moved into the dock with me). 'Take the defendant upstairs. I expect an apology when I resume at two-fifteen.'

He gets up and rushes to his door and I yell out loud as I'm being led away. 'Not only are you a cockhead, you're also an overpaid, lazy, bald-headed, four-eyed, lazy prick.'

He turns, standing now, and says, 'Get him out of here…remanded in custody, a date to follow. A bail assessment report to follow.' He turns to the clerk and says, 'Make a note of that, madam reporter.'

He walks away and I'm led up the stairs.

62

John Downley

The senior magistrate rang the line marked 'Department of Public Prosecutions'. 'John Downley speaking.'

'Yes, Your Honour. How can I help?'

'How's my case coming along, Bill?'

'I'll send you an email.'

'What are the charges now?'

'Four counts of indecent assault.'

'You'll hear from my lawyer.'

The senior magistrate put the phone down and wiped the sweat from his brow. And held his right hand, which shook a trifle more nowadays. He brooded about the so-called victim and said to himself, 'How did I get in this mess?'

Mavis

Before the caps with black and white check bands massed outside of her front window; before the gavel banged with its sharp sound fracturing the emotion-charged atmosphere of the courtroom; before the magistrate pronounced his careful words, Mavis Allen was just an ordinary housewife surrounded with piles of ironing (which brought her pittance money from grateful neighbours), an abusive yet hardworking husband, a daughter and two grandchildren, living in middle-class Australia.

Her life was about to change with her husband's arrest, conviction and a gaol term to follow on a cold bleak day in June 2000 in Adelaide, the capital city of South Australia.

Mavis's mind was in a turmoil: problems were mounting steadfast, almost out of control, and they shook her foundations, which were built on wish, hope and prayer. It was a maxim she adhered to and her words were carefully chosen, delivered in a filtered manner, strained at times, especially in the beginning, percolated as in a coffee pot till they bubbled over, with her words flying out, escaping like an outpouring of champagne from a bottle. They were devoid of swallows, devoid of moisture, evaporated like desiccated coconut, till in the last delivery when she became silent. Her eyes betrayed nothing while she waited for a response from her inner being. (She always thought there were twin souls operating inside her mind.)

Nothing came on that day as she walked towards the northern suburbs bus stop, missing her yoga classes which kept her size twelve figure trim and neat.

She wondered of late how disturbing moments had unglued her thought processes. Had her acceptance of conditions developed into a form of stability? Stability was at the core of her beliefs, though she realised it was a reluctant stability.

Mavis knew she had become insignificant. People either fight or run away when treated with disrespect. Like others in society, the fringe-dwellers who feel no belonging, they wear masks, hoping for a conversion, to be loved by all. And sometimes they put down others, or trample on them, to make themselves feel good.

Mavis never trampled on people less fortunate than herself. She was more spiritually in tune with the universe than her husband.

Her period of silence caused her to reflect on the years of marriage and the mundanity of it all. She knew changes were rushing towards her, even if that rush was like Bob when he would charge in the door, shouting about everything which was wrong in his life and his business. Just like an out of control freight train. The prospect of another twenty years of marriage to Bob with his outbursts had an ending.

It was highlighted when a middle-aged couple boarded the bus and sat in front of her. Their heads touched and their eyes met when they whispered. A sign of what life could be flashed into her mind when she drew a comparison with her life, while the bus trundled on, slow and then fast at times between stops, but always moving forward.

Her brain was flooded with recall of the twenty-nine-year anniversary of some twelve months before. The quiet café: couples dancing to a gypsy violin played softly, with a drunken pianist plonking the keys in the background. Her thick brown hair tinted on the day, nails done. The red dress from her going-away outfit and light make-up (Bob hated her spending money on make-up).

She sipped the white wine while he gulped (as if each was his last drink) five pints of beer, which became tuneful when the belching started. She hoped for a small piece of romance yet her every cell shouted out 'No way.' Sending signs to Bob was not an option; it had been missing in her life for some time.

Bob's rage about everything took over the evening, followed by his six visits to the toilet. He held the floor all night about his unpaid fees.

Mavis came back to the now as the bus trundled along and thought about his outburst to the magistrate, resulting in his being remanded in custody. A shake-up was on the way. Her life had been as clear as a glass of water but now debris had collected at the bottom. A muddied brew seeped into the water: it had been shaken and stirred and a new life was dawning for Mavis Allen.

Mavis walked the two kilometres to her home, glad to be off the bus, no longer watching and eavesdropping on the conversation of the couple in the seat in front. A small tinge of envy had been fashioned as she watched and listened to them, so she needed an escape, a return to the reality of her world.

She studied her face in the reflection in the tinted windows of the bus just before she made the decision to walk. The strain of the last few months showed with black rings under her eyes and the pink dots which appeared over her nose and cheeks when she was under strain. It was diagnosed as a form of acne and her doctor had prescribed some antibiotics.

The parchment-like quality of her face increased as a result of the sleepless nights caused by Bob's snoring; his breath smelled like a brewery. She was never praised for her work in his personal care and in the business. Except at times he said, 'Love your green eyes.' (Which everyone remarked on and which she thought were her best feature.) She no sooner opened her mouth than he would butt in and take over the conversation (just like a goat butting in, her mother used to say).

He was a perfectionist – even with his friends, who were becoming few and far between, because he treated them and his family as if they were employees. When others failed to comply with his every demand, his condemnation was quick and cruel and he would home in on any feature of those folk which created an outburst of laughter. Finally, he would say, 'I should have been on the stage.'

Their last argument ended with a rare fit of remorse at some spiteful words he had shouted. He blurted out, 'I couldn't live without you.'

She was stung, yet she mustered up a reply designed to fight back and yelled, with spittle foaming around her lips. She had saved all her moisture for her good one-liner: 'So why aren't you dead yet?'

Bob turned his back towards her, grabbed the car keys and kicked the front door open, removing another patch of varnish.

Two hours later she heard the car revving, stopping with doors being half slammed and shut again and his footsteps crunching on the gravel outside of the front door. She heard him fumbling for the keys, dropping them and swearing. Then he broke into a giggle.

The door was kicked and Mavis opened it at the same moment, causing him to fall on his back, where he lay on the inside doormat in a pool of urine (from his indelicate bladder). He was snoring within seconds and she threw a blanket from the lounge over his inert form.

Mavis reached for the antidepressants and in the morning her eyes were as wide as saucers. And they did not speak for days.

She brushed that incident out of her mind, counting the steps in her walk towards the street where she lived.

A car door slamming reminded her of the first night when the local cops called. They came to the house from time to time regarding unpaid fines, which she paid, and Mavis knew them by name. Bob used to hide and let Mavis do the dirty work. However, the incident which led to his troubles was a different kettle of fish.

'Open the door, Mavis,' one of them said.

She did not respond.

'We know he's in there. Open it or we'll kick it in.'

'OK, OK,' she replied. It sounded urgent.

Andy the short cop was followed in by his tall partner Brian.

Bob emerged, his face red and full of grog and bravado. He was aggressive. 'Hey, Mavis, looks who's here…Danny De Vito…and Lurch.' Which did not bring any applause from the cops.

Andy moved fast, not speaking. No allegations were delivered, just a grab, a punch swung by Bob without connecting, tipping him off balance, then he was wrapped up in a hold by Andy and propelled out the door, yelling.

'Get Bill the lawyer, Mavis… Hurry up, you stupid cow.'

Bob was bundled in the rear of the police car and was silent all of the journey. He was bailed and returned home sullen and silent at eight a.m. His official papers required him to be at court to answer the charge of 'threatening life' and an added one of 'resisting arrest'. The major charge concerned a contractor who had not paid Bob's bill; Bob had taken matters in his own hands.

He showed Mavis the papers.

'Bloody hell, Bob. It says here you threatened to kill him. Burn his house down, kill his kids if he doesn't pay.'

'Lies, all lies,' he said.

However, she knew when he was lying to her as he always walked away and refused to speak about it. Her words followed him into the bathroom, where he grabbed a towel and a radio. She knew the reason why he always carried out that ritual. Though this time it was in the daytime rather than at night.

'You need help, Bob…and quick.'

Her words were silenced by the sound of the shower turned on full blast and the radio locked on his favourite station. But she could still hear the noise of 'Ah, ah, ah, ah' as – mocking her, she felt – he jerked off under the shower.

The Warrant: Second Non-appearance

Mavis peered through the venetian blinds three weeks after Bob's attendance at court after his first arrest. She did not attend on that occasion, preferring Bob and the lawyer to do the talking. Bob was required to be at court to answer the bail the second time but forgot to tell Mavis the date. His lawyer was interstate. He remembered the date but did not choose to notify the police. A warrant was on that occasion issued for his non-attendance and he knew the cops would show.

He turned off the lights and the TV, and parked his van in the garage.

Mavis saw the same two cops walking towards the front door with official papers in their hands. It was the second time they had checked the darkened house since the warrant was issued by the court. She coughed near the window when the dust flew up from the parting of the blinds and reminded herself they would have to be cleaned.

Constable Andy Duggan banged on the front door after climbing up the two steps. He was short for a cop – five feet six inches – yet what he lacked in height was compensated by his being a martial arts expert.

Senior Constable Brian Jones was six feet six inches and he stood back watching his partner do the work. Brian was head and shoulders above everyone, even at school, and because of his size was never threatened. Sometimes by sheer bluff, he survived any challenges which were cast his way. However, he felt uneasy about arresting the violent Bob Allen for breach of bail.

Brian followed his partner in through the door, which Mavis had opened. He stood and watched (out of striking space) when his partner Andy ducked the punch Bob swung. Bob knew the weak link was

Brian and he brushed Andy aside with his strong frame, determined to get a hit in on one of the officers. Brian caught the giant fist of the tough, hardened bricklayer full on his right ear and then another one in the face. He toppled over like a house of cards and was about to receive a kick in the ribs when Andy blocked the kick, knocking Bob to the ground. Andy handcuffed him on one wrist and clamped the other on his hand.

Brian sat on the front inner doormat still holding his reddened ear.

'Get out of the doorway. I'm coming through.'

Brian struggled to his feet and trotted out, meekly opening the rear door of the police car. Brian drove to the Holden Hill Police Station and Bob was thrust into a padded cell.

The duty sergeant, who knew Bob, spoke to him through the opening. 'I'll let you out if you calm down.'

Bob nodded and he was charged at the charging desk.

'You may speak to a duty lawyer in the morning. You won't be bailed and will appear in the court. Do you understand?'

Once again Bob nodded. And collected a blanket for the night.

He was released from court later in the day after his lawyer put forward features of his business and said that he was not a flight risk.

Before he left the dock, the senior magistrate said, 'You are in a lot of trouble, Mr Allen. There are fresh charges against you and they're quite serious. It appears you have an anger management problem. I advise you to leave your attitude in the foyer before you enter this court again. The next senior magistrate might not be as kind as me. And that will be your third appearance. If you play up, you will be remanded in custody.'

Bob never heeded advice from anyone – not even magistrates. It was to be his undoing.

Mavis

Mavis sighed after they had gone…released the next day. Thank God for small mercies, she muttered when she ploughed through the ironing pile. Bob had turned out just like her father and if her mother was alive she would agree. Her father would have a row with his wife and rush off to the pub for a skinful returning later drunk and looking for sex. She heard the words of her mother in the mid-sixties.

'Donny Dunstan got something right. He ditched six o'clock closing.'

Mavis would stare with a faraway look in her eyes, vowing to never repeat her mother's mistake. Determined never to marry a man like her father.

She sang while she ironed, 'Dashing away with a smoothing iron', and watched as the crease came alive in an almost art form, listening to the rabbit stew cooking on the Metters gas stove. Her thoughts returned about Bob pestering her for sex after she had her operations and how Bob had turned into a scrooge, checking every item she bought at the supermarket. A loving father, she admitted, but now an absolute control freak. She smiled to herself when she showed him the photo she had snapped of him asleep snoring with a lemon which she had placed in his mouth.

'God, I look like a pig,' he remarked.

'You said it, not me,' she replied.

*

'Are you there, Mum?' Lorraine called out.

'Yes, dear. Door's unlocked. Come in.'

Lorraine stood there looking at her mum. They were like peas in a pod: good features, brown hair and green eyes. Lorraine was well dressed (better than her mum); Clarrie, her husband, saw to that. He was generous and had bought her a new car.

'How's Clarrie, love?'

'Good, Mum, good,' swinging the new car keys on her fingers. 'What time is Dad getting home from court?'

'Soon, love. Soon, I expect.'

'Bloody hell…what is wrong with him?'

'Dunno, love. Maybe you can talk to him. My words don't work. You could always wind him round your fingers.'

'Bit late for him to listen to me, Mum.'

Mavis spoke words which she had never used before. 'He's always after me for a root, you know.'

'What! You're still recovering from the ops.'

'Doesn't worry him. Still he's given up…found something else to do.'

'Such as, Mum?' There was a hint of concern in her voice.

'He takes a towel and a radio and jerks off in the shower,' Lorraine spluttered.

'Why the radio? Keep in time, I suppose. Ten strokes and you go blind.'

'Masks the noise, love.'

The front door opened and Bob walked in bright and without anger in his face, as if he was a man who had just won a marathon. He hugged his daughter and just touched Mavis on the head. 'Going to the shower,' and he grabbed a radio.

Mavis winked at her daughter and once the radio blared with the shower on full blast they crept near the door and heard the sounds. 'Ah, ah, ah, ah.'

Lorraine started to giggle.

'See, I told you so, love.'

Both women crept back to the kitchen.

'Gotta go, Mum.'

'See yah, Lorry,' her father yelled.

'Yeah, see ya, Dad,' she called back. Then added, 'Don't forget to turn up at court. This is the third time, I reckon. Take your toothbrush, Dad.'

Her father did not answer.

Lorraine started her new car and adjusted the mirror. 'Jeez, hope Clarrie doesn't get that desperate.'

Clarrie would be preparing a good meal for her when she arrived home after picking up the kids from swimming lessons.

'My, how things can change in a generation,' she whispered while she pondered on the drive home how fortunate her life was. It was a blessed life. A life without flaws…as she often remarked, with a hint of arrogance, to her single-mum divorced friends.

There was Clarrie, personable, helped all who needed, didn't smoke, a moderate drinker, liked his work as a travelling sales rep…away five days and back on weekends. He loved his two girls, who were currently at swimming classes and going well. Never spoke about his parents, though – it was if they never existed. No photos, no memorabilia, and money seemed to be there all the time. Where it came from, no one knew. Lorraine was happy not to enquire about their wealth. She was pleased with her comfortable life and the freedom which she enjoyed. Clarrie did not surround her with a fence like her father did to Mavis.

Lorraine turned into the darkened driveway, which was unusual, as Clarrie was always home from his travels by four p.m. on Fridays. She alighted from her car to be confronted by a woman about thirty years of age carrying a four- or five-year-old girl. She was slender, with light brown hair, and well dressed (as was the child). Her looks were much the same as Lorraine.

She spoke with a hint of anxiety in the voice, 'Is Clarrie home?'

Lorraine paused and thought about her words, her imagination racing out of control, and replied in a sharp manner, 'No. Do you know him?'

'I ought to – we're married This is his daughter. I'm June.'

Lorraine's knees buckled and she reached out, clutching the open car door. It would not hold her and she fell on the driveway.

The woman helped her to her feet. 'I've been following him. Who are you?'

Lorraine mustered up an answer which cracked out into the night air. 'I'm his wife.'

Both women stood together, unable to speak. The silence between them was broken when a rustling noise came from the large native shrubs which Clarrie had planted after they were married. It was followed by a sneeze. Lorraine flashed the key-ring torch which Clarrie had given to her on their last anniversary. Both women saw the crouching form of Clarence Mario Martin on all fours and at the same time the child rushed forward and jumped on his back calling out, 'Daddy. Daddy.' His face was pale and words would not come out.

Lorraine spoke with the bitter edge of a woman scorned and they flew into the dusky evening like a raised sword held high. 'You… dirty…lying…cheating bastard.' She turned, walked into the house, slamming the door. She yelled through the open front window, 'And don't come back.'

June grabbed the child in her arms and spoke her words of hate enunciated with gaps, the same as Lorraine. 'You…fucking…prick.' She turned and fled with tears streaming down her face.

Clarrie stood, brushed off the debris from his Italian suit and walked into the driveway. He started his twin-cab Nissan and drove away, out of the lives of Lorraine and the two daughters who he never saw again.

Clarrie

Alfredo Mario Martino was born in Queensland in 1960. He was the only child of northern Italian parents who had emigrated to Australia after the end of World War Two. They were aristocratic people, rumoured to share the bloodlines of the Borgias from the middle ages, and both were born near the Austrian border. Apart from their pale olive skin, they bore no resemblance to the southern Italian folk, who they looked down on, stamping their heels on the ground like the foot of the Italian peninsula in a well known put-down of their countrymen.

Land was available at cheap prices on the Gold Coast and they purchased many blocks as well as real estate. Other investments caused their bank balances to grow and in a short time they were very wealthy people. Their wealth enabled them to send their son to a boarding school which was managed by Jesuit priests. Apart from extensive gifts, they provided nothing in the way of real love to their only child. It sowed the seeds which fashioned his life in an inappropriate manner. The formal education coupled with a strong feeling of abandonment twisted his thought processes. He knew from an early age he could buy love, and used gifts of money to assist him on his journey. He became an industrial chemist after his university studies provided him with a career and later on a hobby.

The parents returned to their beloved Alps in 1980 and he never cared to see them again. They ensured he would inherit much of their vast holdings and he made good use of his inheritance. He changed his name to Clarence Mario Martin and moved to Adelaide after a five-year stint in his profession.

Bible teachings stuck in his mind and in particular the Hebrews who had many wives, which he thought was a good idea. To be surrounded by love. Two wives would do, he added to himself one night, and from that pivotal moment of insight he set in action a plan.

He met Lorraine Allen at a dancing class (he was a good dancer) and she very quickly fell in love with the five foot ten inch man with the solid build, tanned skin and flashing white teeth which always showed when he smiled – which was almost permanently. The good manners, his taste in food: she knew she had met Mr Right and it was not long before they were married.

He loved his two girls (as much as he could in a superficial fashion) and poured many gifts on them as they grew. He always had an escape route planned yet he had no need to implement it…he was a so-called travelling salesman, on the road from Monday to Friday, home on weekends. No chance of being caught. Just keep the money coming in.

Clarrie had a huge bush block at Sedan just south of the River Murray. The block contained a one-bedroom shack and massive sheds and he would spend all of the week growing the weed and manufacturing drugs. Wealth came from the sales of drugs and from his real estate holdings throughout Australia. No one knew of him and no complaints were made; therefore there were no restrictions on his marketing of the goods.

Within a few years, June came under his radar and in time they married. He was happy with his life, which never showed any signs of changing on the horizon, until the fateful night of confrontation.

Clarrie lay prone on the damp old bitumen with blood oozing out from his wounds. Dribbling, bubbling blood issued from his mouth, his nose and his ears. He hardly heard the thunder and lighting on the road which led to Sedan because it was masked by the dull thuds of the Doc Marten black boots which were being rained on his body. A cracking noise of a broken rib which was laced with the sound of insane shrieking giggles came from the lips of the young blonde woman with tattoos and her huge male partner.

His pain was dulled with the loss of blood yet he was unable to cough up the blood gathering within his throat. He thought about the Jesuits and what they said about sins with the frequent quoting of the Scriptures.

He murmured one of his favourites from the Gospel of Thomas, 'If you bring forth what is within you, what you bring forth will save you. If you do not, what you do not bring forth will destroy you.' And as each blow struck he knew he was close to death. 'Women, sex,' his bubbled lips spoke, and it had undone him again. He hadn't been able to resist the enticing young woman who flagged him down in his twin cab. Then the blow from behind from the man. The sounds of beer can rings being pulled out from the cans in his car. Stupid sounds of burping and gulping.

His eyes closed and peace came upon him with one final puff of breath. It started to pour with heavy rain.

The two assailants hid under a large red gum tree branch just off the road and watched the lightning flashes. They hardly heard the lightning bolt which struck the tree and them. In their last moments they yelled out 'Oh shit!' in unison before they were reduced to a steaming pile of ashes.

Clarrie whooshed out of his body and watched the scene below – as well as the ascent of the two thugs who screamed on their new journey upwards.

*

Detective Sergeant Rollison picked his way carefully over the scene with the crime scene examiner.

'What do you think, Geoff?'

Senior Constable Geoff Matthews lit up his pipe, which was always somewhere within his reach. It was upside down because of the heavy rain. However, he was able to still keep it alight. 'Des, it's bloody biblical.'

'What?'

'The two piles of ashes you see under the tree were struck by a lightning bolt – they still have cans of VB and a wallet in them.'

'Kicked to death, I think – broken ribs, nose all over. Loss of blood – by them, I reckon.'

Des thought about his Sunday school days and retribution. He shook his head and said, 'Jeez, you're right.'

'There's more – look at the two photos in the wallet. Young women with kids. One has two girls, the other a toddler. The photos are in separate folders.'

Des fingered the photos. 'Unless they're sisters, I'd say our dead man on the road, Clarence Martin, by what I can make out, has two separate families. Naughty boy.'

Des drove off, leaving the body people to guard the scene and others to preserve it (when it stopped raining). He sat in his car and spoke to himself. 'Bloody flaws in all of us,' and he remembered his father, who had shot through to Thailand with a young woman. His mother died of cancer shortly after. He never forgave his dad. 'It's all bloody grey. Forget the black and white.' It was a saying he frequently used. He had read a verse from an unknown spruiker which said, 'Every saint has a past, and every sinner has a future.'

John's Case

The two lawyers played every Friday after work on the North Adelaide Golf Course. It had been their custom for many years, since they both graduated from law school. Bill moved into the Department of Public Prosecutions and Sam stayed with criminal law in a well known Adelaide firm as a defence counsel.

Golf was a welcome break for the men and they were able to discuss, informally, matters which concerned them both. Sam was appearing for John Downley; the case of indecent assault was in the early stages.

They were nearing the end of the course when Sam opened up about his client John, the magistrate. 'Where are we at at this moment with JD, Bill?'

'Stuck for a while. The victim's overseas and may not be coming back.'

'This was two years ago, mate…any corroboration?'

'She saved her pantyhose with the beans still attached.'

'Clever girl…another Monica…shades of Bill Clinton.'

Bill was silent while he drove the ball and they walked on. 'Maybe, mate. Maybe.'

'So. Four counts. Tell me about it.'

'She was his clerk and he had a thing about her.'

'Can't say I blame him…she was a smasher in those tight, short skirts.'

'He's a judicial officer, supposed to keep a tight reign on his cock…'

'OK, OK. What then?'

'He corners her in his chambers while she's sitting on his desk and peers up her skirt.'

'Yes.'

'He pats her on the head and his arms slips to her breast, which he fondles.'

Sam was silent.

'He moves in close and pulls out the old kidney wiper and starts to feed the chooks while she moves back, but she's trapped and he lets it all go over the pantyhose.'

'What else?'

'This happened three more times but she wasn't on the desk, only half into the door. He managed a grope of her breast and her crotch till she fled. Then she resigned.'

'When did she complain?'

'About eighteen months later.'

'So what now?'

'We have the smeared article and we'll ask him for a DNA test if she proceeds.'

'Not considering suspending him at this stage?'

'No. But the chief maggie knows a bit about it.'

'So what do you want me to tell him?'

'Look, mate, it will all come out. She might go to the press, you know.'

'Always a worry, isn't it? Still, I will have to tell him something.'

'If she insists, and I think she will, get him to plead guilty. Saves it all being dragged out in court. He's out then, no more senior magistrate – but I'm sure the judge would take all of it into account. Maybe twelve months on the bottom.'

Sam walked ahead and placed his ball on the tee and drove a straight shot.

'Bugger,' said Bill, who was always beaten by Sam.

'Let's have a drink and talk some more later after I've talked to John, OK?'

The two old friends walked to the club and ordered beers. Sam was on light beer. His licence had only been just restored after blowing .055 a while ago.

Mavis

Mavis was spring cleaning in her bandana, her housecoat pockets spilling over with cleaning rags, the hoover roaring, the phone off the hook. She wanted no interruptions while on the mission she had vowed some twelve months ago to accomplish. So much had happened in that time and she thought about the sequence of dramas which had unfolded.

The terrible news about Clarrie, his betrayal and his murder. The double life which shattered his wife (wives is more appropriate, she thought). The kids suffering at the funeral and sadness that hung about for weeks until the will came out and Lorraine was suddenly a wealthy woman (not from the drugs but from the properties). The phone call much later from Lorraine, who had taken the kids on a holiday to Darwin.

'Mum. Met another man. Army major. Soon to retire. A bit older than me. Wants me to live with him here in Darwin. Kids like him. His are grown up. I might. Maybe a bit soon, though.'

Mavis mused. Her daughter always got up after falling down and she knew they would live out there. And she did. The kids adjusted and love it.

No more talk of Clarrie, though Bob would not hear a bad word about him.

Of course there was Bob, now in gaol. John Downley gave him two years. Minimum eighteen months parole. There were other men Bob threatened who came out of the woodwork. Mavis did not attend court when Bob was sentenced. She let Sam do the speaking and Bob shut up as he was told. She did not wish to hear any more of Bob's embarrassing outbursts and, besides, they were now separated – while he was in gaol anyway.

Then the most surprising news. The magistrate John Downley was arrested and pleaded guilty to indecent assault. He got eighteen months in the same prison as Bob. 'My, my,' she thought, 'how the mighty have fallen. Don't like his chances of surviving if he's in a cell near Bob.'

The phone rang after the hoover was switched off.

'Mum. The kids send their love. Have you seen Dad?'

'No. Don't intend to. We're formally separated.'

'Why?' There was a sharp edge to Lorraine's tone.

'Look, you're doing your thing. All of a sudden Miss Wealthy Pants is doing OK. I'm doing my thing, all right?' She heard Lorraine breathing and thinking.

'Sorry, Mum. I was out of line. You're right. Twenty more years with him would probably kill you. Keep me posted and come up some time. I'll send you a plane ticket.'

'OK, love. Catch you later.'

John Downley

John looked around his sparse cell in Yatala Labour Prison at Northfield in Adelaide's northern suburbs and saw the minimum luxuries of books and a laptop. The girl who had complained was happy when John pleaded guilty and received a shorter sentence. He knew every inch of his close quarters, which he had surveyed frequently during his incarceration. So much had happened and the earth had circled the sun in that time. He was watched over constantly because of his protected status. When he was out and in the fresh air, he saw the angry eyes of other inmates shouting, always shouting, the same chant over and over, 'Dog… Dog… Dog.' That lasted for three months and stopped abruptly.

The nights were the enemy, when the dreams came. A persistent dream of being in a deep canyon with mossy sides. He was unable to climb out and fearful of falling into a fiery pit where demons lurked with three-pronged spears being thrust towards him with gnarled old fingers, and arms with tattoos dotted.

He sweated, tossing and turning, until morning, when the shaving started. The mirror stared back at him and the face was pale, and dotted with lumps. He negotiated the blade between the lumps, changing hands because of the tremor, which told of an early stage of Parkinson's disease.

The careful ritual made him think he had become like a retreaded tyre which had developed a bulb. The bulb grew with thousands of revolutions until the flopping sound of wear faded. The tread fell apart and motion ceased. Will I fall apart in a flash while I'm shaving and the guards rush in spotting foam coming out of my mouth? Will I ever get another retread? Must I search for my retread or will it never happen?

His thoughts circled around and always came back to his marriage to Judy. Career, marriage and disgrace ended his venture. However, before the nightly ending, before Judy made her move, before the onset of the trembling hands, he remembered their final words to each other, which were dripping with poison.

Judy had within her mind a series of venomous outbursts which when delivered stabbed at his heart. She knew when, where and how to turn the screw. The worst moment came in the bedroom after a social event with friends.

'Close the blinds, Jude.'

'Why? You like the light. So you tell me.' She had developed a style of answering with a question, followed by a nasty little titbit.

He fumbled in a drawer while he selected a pair of short pyjamas. 'Don't want the neighbours to spot my knackers.'

A twisted sneer flooded her face: he had seen that expression many times and he surmised that if she swallowed a nail she would probably shit a corkscrew.

Judy drew into her lungs the smoke from the expensive cigarette. She stared at him without blinking and, knowing he hated smoking, puffed out a cloud of blue smoke which drifted over his face. Then she spoke carefully with two words. 'What knackers?'

And that was the moment when he knew it was over. A moment when he watched her walk away humming, with a smile on her lips. He knew he had to leave. The charges came along, as did the tremors; the marriage was over with no hope of a re-match.

His dreams continued in the cell. However, he made an offer to teach inmates the law. It was a chance to resume what he knew best – teaching – and it kept the daytime hours full and rewarding.

Among the students was Bob Allen, whom the former respected judicial officer had sentenced before his fall. Bob spoke to him after a class and said, 'No hard feelings, judge. I went off the rails and you did what you had to.'

Bob became a receptive student, asking sensible questions, and seemed to be turning his previous nature around. Yet a look would flood his features on occasions which sent John a note of caution. However, he could not see inside of the mind of Bob Allen. He could not know of the cunning which had developed, or the dusty spaces within his mind; the unfounded assumptions concerning the judge who had ruined his life and the plans which were being hatched.

Mavis

Mavis never imagined that divorce would occupy her thoughts. Lorraine, their only child, who had presented her with two beloved grandchildren, could not contemplate a permanent break with her parents, who would have to divide up all the hard-earned assets, the cars, the business, the accumulated super, the photos and the memories, which would be stowed away forever in some unloved suitcase with no significance to strangers and no idea of what traumas it had cost to accumulate such possessions.

Yet Lorraine had embarked on her journey with one eye cast back towards her mother and her father, who she knew was an unstable mix of serious, personal and explosive, all lumped together in an unusually incompatible mix – like broccoli and peaches – a man who might one day kill her mother.

Mavis sensed her daughter wished her happiness, although not too much of it. After all, a rock sits unmoving (and her mother was a rock) and asks for nothing more than to watch the change of seasons.

What would Mavis's diminishing circle of friends have to gossip about after a break in the marriage? Those thoughts prowled in Mavis's mind. Would it be a collection of sharpened knives? Would it be a slicing, a traducing, a reducing of flesh because of Bob's cancer – with no one to care for him in his last hours? Yet it was said to be in remission. Did she need the advice of friends who did not sleep in her bedroom? Her therapist had a different view and he suggested that freedom, and her own need and search, were the issue. Bob had made his choices. She needed to break the bond. A search for meaning in her life was paramount.

The yoga teacher breathed sound advice which was loaded with ancient wisdom such as 'Don't search for the meaning of life. It is not under a rock or in a cave. Just move forward, always noticing, and if you die in the process, well, that's cool. At least you won't die of boredom.'

Mavis considered her mother's wise sayings. Like 'Let life happen instead of making it happen which creates a resistance to waiting.'

'What do you mean, Mum?' the sixteen-year-old had said.

'Signs, love…signs, dreams will tell you…prayer helps.'

'OK,' the bored teenager had said.

'We should be like bulbs…be a mystery…wait for the layers to peel off instead of picking them off. Know what I mean?'

'Yeah…I think so, Mum.'

And waiting became the dominant feature of the many years in her marriage to Bob.

Yet of late, since his time in gaol, fortuitous events caused her to plan after some signs were sent in dreams. She had changed and, rather than waiting like a bulb in the moist productive soil, taking each day and spending it in the now, she bit the bullet after a phone call from Bob out of the blue.

The curiosity in her voice spiked and she spoke. 'Why, Bob?'

'I'm off to Coober Pedy. Mining. Always wanted to do it. Going with John Downley.'

Mavis gasped yet thought of an answer. 'The judge who gaoled you.'

'Yep. Taught us all law in gaol. He's got some dough stashed. We can buy a lease.'

She thought on his words, which made the marriage irretrievable.

'Bob, I did some research on the Allen family. Let me know your address and I'll send it to you, OK?'

'Thanks, I'll read it later. See ya.' The phone call ended.

Mavis sat and cried for a full ten minutes until her tear ducts dried. Thirty-odd years vanished; the rock of her marriage had fallen into a canyon. She knew the inevitable divorce would follow and the good times would be blackened. She knew the divorce would violate the present and desecrate the past. The good would lurch away stumbling like a train guard who had survived a train wreck. Yet she had to move on forward, always forward.

She shook herself like a wet dog and walked towards the bulky, unopened parcel tied with red ribbons, and read the bracketed words 'The Family Tree of Allen: five hundred pages of dedicated research.' It remained unopened where it sat, on the hall table, until the forwarding address arrived, when it was sent to Coober Pedy.

Bob left the parcel intact from the time he received it. He had more on his mind.

Coober Pedy

The mounds and mounds of pale mullock which surround the opal mining town of Coober Pedy have been deposited over the decades by successive waves of hopeful diggers trying their luck on Australia's richest opal field in the desert outback of South Australia. Opal veins occur as deep as thirty metres below the surface, randomly distributed in clay banks sandwiched between layers of sandstone. And anyone with a prospecting permit has a chance of striking it rich either by sinking a shaft or noodling into the surface through the piles of unwanted waste. The miners have adapted to the fifty-degree heat by living in shelters underground. It is twenty-four degrees in those shelters, and churches and all manner of housing have been carefully dug out over the years. Air shafts to the surface provide light and a comfortable living.

The two former gaol mates with vastly different backgrounds joined the miners in the search for riches and a different lifestyle. John and Bob welcomed the change of pace. However, one of them had a much more serious plan in mind.

Bob Allen drove his partner John Downley's near-new Nissan turbo diesel, towing a new trailer. They were travelling north towards Coober Pedy, which might provide an adventure, spliced with back-breaking work, long hours with the prospect of striking layers of fine-quality opals.

'How are you, judge?' Bob enquired about the tremor in his hands which came on after protracted periods of sitting.

'Tablets help, but seriously, I don't know how long I have on the planet. Hence the sea change.'

Bob nodded. He was quieter nowadays and owed it to the long

hours in a cell where he had to examine his life. Those moments of examination did not alter his deeper thoughts about the man who had ruined his life. He enjoyed the game of outwitting and toying with a man of great intelligence. However, he smirked when he knew his level of cunning did not match the IQ.

Bob's ego never missed a beat and many shrinks would have diagnosed him with a highly developed form of dissonance which was under control. The game boosted his ego and he spoke, of late, with a clinical air as if discussing how to boil an egg. He banished his unwanted thoughts, like Mavis, the wife who had abandoned him in his hour of need. His daughter Lorraine was slotted in the same folder as her mother because she did not visit him in gaol. He knew those thoughts were long past their use-by date. And he was comfortable with his current style of examining his rage without allowing it to take over. He did not fear that it would re-engage and once again control his emotions. The judge was a different fish, because he held those thoughts deep down in the bowels of his body and they simmered away like bubbling lava. Yet still he ignored the central question. How did he arrive at this point in his life? He was always in denial, with his steps paving the way to his own downfall, and lobbing the blame on the judge.

Despite his inner refusal to confront the issue of forgiveness and small voices in the night (which would whisper, 'Sooner or later'), it remained trapped in a cocoon, until the revelations would reveal the words and the truth behind them. Bob surmised that, sooner or later, it would mean the last act of vengeance, which he had not explored on the other side of those evocative words. The egocentric man never understood that his manner drove family and friends into desperate reactions.

Bob broke the silence in the cabin as they negotiated a bend in the road. 'What about your wife?'

'The ending – well, couldn't stand her cruel comments actually.'

'Yeah – though my Mavis was usually silent. Relationships start out OK, gold and glitter, but become tarnished. Most of us settle for gilded. Dressed up for appearance's sake, I suppose.'

Bob plucked a nose hair from his nose and sneezed in the process, screwing up his face like a man who had swallowed a glass of vinegar. The sneeze caused them to veer into the path of an oncoming truck and they narrowly avoided a collision, with the other driver swearing and blowing the horn.

'Shit, judge. Better pull over.'

John passed over a can of beer and Bob took a swig and licked his lips.

'Ahh, the tears of a goddess.'

John chuckled at his partner's recent turns of phrase and then thought about what he would say. 'Bob, I've altered the will. You'll get the rig, OK?'

'Thanks, judge.' Bob contained his excitement yet a thought circled: 'I'm really in control now.'

'Jude still gets half the house when it's sold and in time the daughter will get the lot.'

'You might outlive me, judge, you know.'

'Doubt it, mate…doubt it. You also get the lease.'

They drove into the mining town and found their dugout very easily. In a matter of weeks they had sorted out their working relationship for the mining tasks and other chores.

*

John stood at the edge of the deep shaft as he watched the bright stars blinking their Morse code. His mind was free now because of turning points and spiritual books which he had absorbed in the lonely hours in his cell. The dreams of drama, confusion and fragmented thoughts of regret were gone, replaced with a redemption dream which clearly overtook the old nightmares. Lights of many hues flitted in and they were like a lighthouse with a three-hundred-and-sixty-degree gyration with a healing light shining on his body adding to his visions of wondrous light. He wondered if it was the light of God.

His former belief system of certain standards, in order to feel good about himself, caused an unconscious form of self-adulation, which over time had created a window of self-delusion. The social circle of friends, all tied up with symbolic religion and words muttered without meaning, followed by screeching voices singing hymns without meaning, caused a recall. It sounded like drunks at a pub with a karaoke machine. When the boring pastor had finished, they flocked outside and gossiped about anyone in the vicinity with long hair or too-short hair, and pregnant young mothers. Then it was politics, racial overtones and the sinful use of God's name in vain.

John muttered his last prayer to God on the night of those twinkling stars shining down to his feet at the edge of the deep shaft. The sounds of footsteps slowly creeping from behind caused him to turn round.

Bob stood close and John focused on his face with the lips twisted in an expression he had not seen since the day he sent him to gaol. He saw a huge rock held high by muscular arms which were plunged down. John tumbled, in great pain from the top of his head. Blood poured from him and in seconds he had hit the bottom of the shaft, bouncing once, twice, and then lay inert with twisted limbs splayed at awkward angles. His breath had escaped from his body and he was in the act of passing onto another plane of existence. He would not have heard Bob yell, 'Sooner or later.' Yet the tremor of his right hand persisted for a short time.

The killer flashed a torch to satisfy himself that the victim was dead. Bob thought about the man who had led him into disgrace and walked away, picking his feet up over the rocks and jingling the car keys of the rig in his jacket pocket.

He picked up the parcel which Mavis had sent and by torchlight ran his fingers over the entries until coming to an entry marked 'Downley', which he read carefully. A gasp of air blew out of his mouth when he read the entry.

John Davis…born Adelaide…mother Blanche Davis.
John Davis adopted at birth by James and Mary Downley.
Blanche married later to Brian Allen. Bore a son Bob Allen.

Bob sat back shaking like a dog who had swallowed a razor blade
and he held his head in his hands as the reality bit. The pain came in
waves. It was like sprinkling sulphur on an open wound, nipping at
first like a bee sting which turned into a throbbing mess of skin, torn
flesh and protruding white bones.

The tears came fast and flooding with the white dusty wind
streaking his face like two cans of unmatched paint not thoroughly
mixed. He sat down under control for a second, and wrote on a piece
of paper which he attached with a glider clip to the Allen document:'I
killed my brother.'

He trudged back to the mine with a water bottle and a phial full
of sleeping tablets and sat on the edge. He swallowed the tablets and
washed them down with the water.

A short time later he also was inert and dead, in the arms of John
Downley, a brother he never knew. How different their lives might
have been if they had grown together. It would have given them some
support against a violent father.

*

The stench of rotting flesh and flies led to the discovery of the bodies
and in time the coroner pronounced his decision of murder/suicide.

The coroner was a former friend of John's and after his address he
walked into his chambers, pulled out a bottle of Johnny Walker Black
Label and sat drinking, drink after drink until he was at the point of
vomiting. He rang his secretary and with slurred words said, 'Jean, can
you ring Mary and ask her to pick me up. I'm too pissed.'

Jean obeyed as she always did, for she was in love with her boss,
though she never revealed her feelings.

Mavis

The service for Bob was held in the Methodist church near our house. Not that we ever attended there, though Lorraine went to Sunday school. I had my views. Bob believed in oblivion yet at times he was spooked when he reckoned he saw his father staring at him in the mirror which was Bob's favourite place. His macho ego would stare for hours in the full-length mirror, where he would practise expressions to be used on employees and clients who did not pay up on time. After an hour or so, he would emerge with his neatly combed hair and the bucket hat on his head. His white shirt with the sleeves cut out revealed muscular arms.

The enormous number of chin-ups he did each night gave him a back as wide as a barn door and it was always flexed, especially if a woman walked past. At the end of a day of flexing, he could hardly put his arms to the side. The tape measure was used to measure his forty-seven-inch chest, a measurement which I think he fudged a bit. Then of course there were the liberal doses of aftershave leaving him smelling like a French poof.

Our social life had just about gone and then there was the saga of Clarrie and all the stuff which came with it.

The suicide/murder of the judge some weeks after their release sent me to a therapist, which helped. But I was worn out by too much information and I lay in the double bed at home. I heard a loud bang from the lounge and carefully picked my way to the light switch. Our wedding photo had come off the hook and fallen, smashing the glass. I picked it up and stared at it and a tear formed. I looked around the room but the windows were shut tight, so no wind could have dislodged it. I placed it back on the mantelpiece and then smelled a strong spicy smell.

I tracked the source to the bathroom and then knew what it was. It was Bay Rum, Bob's favourite. A chill embraced my solar plexus and persisted. My teeth rattled and I knew what it was. Bob or some part of him was there in the house. The cold air stopped.

The days passed unnoticed. However, the nights didn't. I had vivid dreams; Bob and I were making love and it was marvellous. It continued for many nights after and I would always wake up yelling, 'Don't leave me, Bob.' Then the advice would come with what to do with my life and I accepted him into my life. Why not? I was on my own. What's wrong with a ghost lover? Not too many complications. No sheets to wash afterwards.

My spooky friend Sue thought otherwise and told me so one day after we caught up. (I had phoned her about Bob and his spirit.)

'He's possessing you. It's dangerous.'

'There's a message somewhere in this, you know.'

'Can't see it,' she replied. 'Let me come over and bless the place. Sage in the corners works with unwanted spirits.'

'But he's wanted, Sue.'

Bob sent signs and I turned on the TV late one night and saw women of all ages and colours driving huge trucks in the north-west of Australia. I made a note to call the phone number and found out it was a TAFE course, which I applied for. The forms came back and I ticked all the boxes. Two weeks later I received approval to attend a course. I passed with flying colours and, more important, Bob approved.

Accommodation was the stumbling block and after a dream I woke up and knew what I would do. I phoned Lorraine in Darwin and told her I was selling the house and going to buy a mobile home. She was enthusiastic. We would both be in the Top End and holidays would be simpler. The house sold quickly and there I was, off like a rocket on the way.

The journey was long and it gave me time to reflect on my life and the chance which I had now taken. Bob had tagged along with me and I was amused that a spirit would have to hitch a ride. However, he told me that he could be in any part of the world within a flash if he wished.

Bob arrived each night around nine p.m. I don't know how he got the timing right as they're not supposed to have watches in the afterlife. Maybe it was the shadows on sticks or something. No photos falling off walls or Bay Rum. I just knew he was about.

Some of my reflections on the past enabled me to see how far I had come. I was a trapped housewife not sure who I was – someone's wife, someone's mother – and prayer back then did not help. Even though I asked for grace on some occasions, I was reminded by a friend that grace cannot be ordered like Hungry Jacks. She also told me that God gave us free will and He's there only to pick us up in times of great stress.

A strange dream persisted for about a week like a continuing miniseries. I was crossing a desert and felt parched. My sweat mingled with the colourful sands and my face looked like a circus clown's. It was a journey which the pedantic Bob would not take. He would be the one who would plan it for weeks. My choice was to rely on the universe to get me through, living day by day and trusting on a good outcome. Being over-optimistic.

With my-sand blasted eyes I saw an oasis in the distance and ran towards the green patches. I entered between two massive hedges and drank cool water from a tumbling waterfall. I gobbled up the dates on the trees. Panic gripped me when I saw I was in a maze and night was coming on fast. I sat with my knees up and arms wrapped around my legs, and memories of my childhood came back. I was the middle child and at times felt I was adopted.

Then Bob appeared. Charming in a suit, he held out his hand and walked with me out of the maze. I realised I had placed my happiness in the hands of another and the following disappointment loomed as a reality and gathered speed.

The dreams stopped and I remembered that talking to him in the last few years was like watching a foreign movie and trying to read the subtitles while matching the mouths of the actors out of kilter with the dialogue.

Those reflections started my path, slowly at first, into reality. I had an earth life to live. Bob was gone, for a time, that is.

I arrived at the site and was made welcome in a warm fashion by the other girls and shown around. Driving tests went on for some time and I was assigned to a senior girl who was helpful and a widow as well.

Friendships grew and prospered and we spoke often.

'I was always hopeful that Bob would get better and never challenged him very much. Maybe I should have.'

Jane said, 'My man was much the same but I miss him now.'

'I tried humour sometimes but it fell on deaf ears. He'd just sit like a paratrooper who was about to fall on a prickly pear.'

The girls all laughed for a while at that one-liner and actually thought I was a bit of a comedian.

Amy spoke. She was the oldest and divorced. 'I always thought that happiness was my rite of passage into old age but it slipped away with Des when he left for a younger woman.'

We were silent in our thoughts as we sipped our Cokes.

Jo spoke. She was usually quiet. 'John always had a far away look in his eyes in between the spaces when he put me down. I was able to counter his remarks and left him each time with some dignity. I was acting like a butler, I reckon. "Would Sir like this or that?"'

'Shit!' we said collectively.

'How did you get on top of him then?' I asked.

'I wouldn't iron his shirts.'

'So now you're here with us…happy?'

'Better than before.'

Amy concluded the conversation with a few words. 'Men…who needs them!'

'Amen to that,' everyone yelled.

I went back to my trailer that night and said in a loud voice, 'Hey, Bob, some people think I'm funny.' There were no wispy shadows that night. I think Bob still has an ego problem.

Judy Downley

Judy sat in her small unit constructed with slabs of bamboo and other gathered materials in Thailand, where she now lived after the murder of her husband John. Despite the yawning chasm between them after she had separated from John (when he went to gaol) and she returned to the house for a brief period until it was sold, she never wished for his death. The shock of his death at the hands of a man he had befriended and trusted hit her with a thud because it was beyond her comprehension.

His fall from grace struck her in a rebound like a basketball bouncing back from a metal hoop. How could a man with such perfect manners and perfect schooling, a careful planner all of his life, be suddenly embroiled in looking up a girl's skirt and masturbating in front of her? He was a judicial officer and they were supposed to be beyond reproach. They were certainly paid enough to keep their heads down. Yet it did no good and there was no closure for her in picking to pieces the reasons why. Hypnotherapy helped but it left her with some of the responsibility for his disgraceful conduct. Of that she was ashamed and she felt she could have handled the breakdown which came on rapidly afterwards.

His initial denials were what she expected yet she knew something was up when she found a dog-eared photo of a nude thirteen-year-old girl tucked in a hidden sleeve of his wallet. She never let on about the discovery, being unsure of what complications it might cause. Her jaw dropped at the spectacle of the photo – along with the penny. It was if she had been asleep during a boring play and woke with a start, clapping before anyone else, with the onlookers gazing at her in silence. Who else knew about his predilections? Her lifelong stammer, which came on in times of stress, had for some reason vanished with the finding of the photo and she knew not why.

Perhaps it was the beginning of the end, with her anxieties melting away just like the meltdown of the marriage. She read a lot more of late and a phrase in a self-help book stuck like wet sand to a bucket. Relationships are like two tuning forks placed next to each other; one adjusts to match the other and if the fit does not work, the harmony of sounds falls flat unless they are rearranged. The harmony had gone.

Thailand loomed because of trips she had made there. She read about the Thais' faith and knew it was an escape for her. A course in the language of those people filled in the obsessive hours when she struggled with her conscience. Her application for work as an English teacher in Thailand was approved and it was her intention to take up the offer; after all, she had thrown away her teaching career to assist John in his legal ambitions. Which in the fullness of time was a mistake.

Judy moved to Thailand and converted to the Buddhist faith with all of its rituals and beliefs, especially re-birth. She felt she had lived many lives and owed John a debt. The debt had been paid and it was time to focus on her new life.

Mavis Allen's and Judy's paths never crossed, although both women had created new lives as a result of spiritual readings, advice and conclusions. Judy had grown to appreciate living one day at a time and never made any plans which could not be altered. She had decided to let God fix her path; whatever obstacles came along could be avoided with God's help.

Then there were the sayings which she wrote in her pink book with angels on the cover: 'Don't keep searching for the truth – just let go of your opinions.'

Judy observed every second and spent time watching the movement of ants and other insects; her powers of observation became sharp and highly regarded by her friends in her new country. Their leader reinforced her beliefs with other messages such as 'The meaning of life is just to move forward and trust in God.' Her prayers were simple. She asked for good health and sent healing to those who she knew needed it. Her daughter knew she was receiving absent healing from her mother and acknowledged it each week with text messages. 'Thanks, Mum. We're well. Take care' was the usual response she received from Australia.

Her walking style had changed. Rather than the heel-toe one-two-three almost like a dance step intermingled with the old athletic netball up on the toes, not a minute to spare, gotta get a goal, she walked with a softer tread in her new fashion. It was almost a shuffle, as if she was caressing the earth's skin.

Vibrations entered through her feet, spreading along the ankles, calves, knees and thighs, moving upward towards the source of life at the base of her spine. Pausing, probing laterally and connecting with the vertebrae, making adjustments on the journey of healing each day, coiling around the seven chakras and finally flowing out of the crown (the seventh). Trapped, harmful waste of old emotions vanished into the atmosphere with their toxic waste disintegrating into the energy waves of nearby trees.

Apart from the pull of her family, she had no intention of returning to suburban Australia with all of its Western materialism. She had become, to all intents and purposes, an ultimate mystic.

As the Buddha said, 'Salvation does not come through the sight of me. It comes from discipline and hard work. So work diligently for your own salvations.'

Mavis

My wages were very good and much of it was stowed away into super. There was not much opportunity to waste money in shopping in the camp and most of us mingled, read books and watched sunsets. The work was dirty, tiring, yet rewarding and I was glad I had made the move.

A detective senior sergeant came to our camp making enquiries. His name was Ken Stock and he was about ten years older than me, with his eye towards retirement. He was intrigued with my mobile home and asked if he could have a look at it. I showed him round and thought then what a good sort he was, tall and slender with brown skin.

He saw the photo of Lorraine and the kids standing with her former army man, now my son-in-law, when they were on a sea cruise.

He looked closely at the photo and smiled. 'Is she your daughter?'

'Yes. With her husband Phil and my grandkids. He's older than me, you know.'

'I've met her. I also know Phil. He was my platoon sergeant in Vietnam years ago.'

I looked at him. 'Well, I'll be buggered.'

'Nothing surprises me in life now. I'll be back this way soon. What say when you get leave we meet up in Darwin?'

'OK… Won't be for a while, though. Got to accumulate some leave.'

We shook hands and he walked away. I watched his posture and thought what a fine-looking bloke he was. I was still amazed at the connection. He turned back and looked at me and I knew then something would develop between us. He waved and smiled back.

I phoned Lorraine that night and told her of our meeting.

'Mum, he's a good bloke. He's a widower, you know. Phil really likes him. We should get together.'

'He's already asked me that.'

'What did you say?'

'First time some bloke has actually asked me out,' I blurted out, 'and said yes.'

'I can't wait to tell Phil. Good for you, Mum.'

'Slow down, girl, slow down.' But I knew how her brain would be racing away.

After dinner Amy said, 'I saw Ken Stock having a look at your home.'

'Yep. Making enquiries. He actually knows my daughter and her husband. They were in Vietnam together. Amazing.'

She smirked and said, 'Good sort, isn't he? Did he say why he was here?'

'No.'

'Probably looking for that dickhead Carter. I saw him duck out of sight when Ken was here.'

Carter was a giant dangerous man who was always skulking around the women. He was rumoured to have raped a few and we were warned off him. He'd make advances, so we kept a healthy distance from him. We couldn't understand how he had got the job. Must have known someone, one of the girls said. He was hated by men and women alike and was some sort of maintenance man who bullied the staff in the workshops.

I avoided him one day when I saw him nearby watching me.

He yelled out in a loud voice, 'Love to see you without clothes.'

I yelled back, 'Forget it, mate. I'm too old for you.'

My retort did not deter him. He always seemed to be near, watching with his big black nasty eyes. Even Bob whispered one night in my dreams, 'Watch Carter.'

I hoped Carter would find better pickings and I forgot about him.

However, he did not forget me. I was close to the end of my shift. It was dusk and I stopped for a comfort break. The diesels were still throbbing and, lost in the glorious fading colours of the red sky, I ambled back to the truck.

I became aware of a presence behind me. It was that feeling one can get in a crowd when you know someone is watching you and you alone. It's when a prickling in the base of the spine occurs (at least, that's my reaction). I turned round to see the giant running towards me with a large black handgun in his hand. I leapt up into the truck and locked the cabin. I pushed the truck into forward and it moved down the incline gathering speed.

He moved fast for a big man, jumping and landing on the short bonnet waving his gun at the windscreen with his scary eyes, shouting, 'Stop, stop.'

But I didn't. The truck picked up speed. He was barely hanging on but he was able to fire a shot into the windscreen. I ducked as the bullet whizzed past my left ear.

The truck was rattling along downhill when I heard Bob's voice. 'Brake now,' he said and I did.

Carter slid off the bonnet and I heard a short scream. I stopped and very gingerly slid down, with my eye on the giant front wheel with blood all over it. I saw his flattened body wrapped around the axle and the wheel. He was as flat as a flounder with brains and bits and pieces of his body littered about. I called for assistance and the supervisor raced up the hill and jumped out of his van.

He looked at the mangled remains of Carter and said one word. 'Shit!'

I was sent to the first aid station. I sat there for some time, and given two days off from work because of shock. Carter's remains were scraped off and put into cold storage.

I heard the sound of a light plane and soon heard voices. Ken was there at my mobile home and I walked out to greet him. He was very professional and asked me if he could tape the interview.

At its completion, he spoke informally to me, asking first how I was. 'Carter has used false names. We've been after him for some time. He shot and killed a man in the Kimberleys and used his ID. Good riddance to bad rubbish, I'd say.'

Ken flew out and we promised to stay in touch. I was exonerated later with a coroner's inquest which was conducted over video link. I became the camp hero. I could do no wrong and the girls threw a party for me. Still, I had killed a man, which is nothing to brag about.

Should I rely on a ghost to keep me out of harm's way? My thoughts were becoming much clearer and I had to be more prudent, trusting my head and not my heart. It was time to bid farewell to Bob (if I could). I had some leave owing now. I ought to visit the mine shaft at Coober Pedy and say a farewell to Bob if his spirit was floating around that town. It seemed appropriate that Bob and I were born on the same day in September and he died in September. We always sang (when we were happy) the old tune 'September'. I hummed it on the light plane when I flew to Coober Pedy.

I stood on the edge of the mineshaft and looked down. It was our birthday and once again I hummed the evocative tune. I was rugged up against the cold and aware of the danger nearby. I tried to imagine the scenario which had ended two lives. My thoughts were interrupted by Bob's familiar whisper close by. Above the noise of the whistling wind, the voice called out, 'Mavis.'

I cocked my ear towards the whisper that seemed to drift on the wind yet had a strange edge to it. Almost like an order. 'Look down, look up. It's easy, don't be scared. Just take a step forward.' It was the clearest message I had heard for weeks and it hit me like a brick. I stepped back carefully from the edge with that human instinct, now raging, for survival. My toes were curled as if to make a stronger foothold.

He wanted me to jump, to be with him, to share his failures. It had been his plan all along. My legs went rubbery and I almost fell down onto the stony surface with my hair blowing into my eyes and tears welling. I was shocked at the gravity of his words and his intentions. I stumbled back to the cave motel and gathered my thoughts with a liberal dose of brandy and Coke. I took hold of myself and felt the warmth coming back into my body. I opened my diary and made a final entry, hoping my writing would provide a closure for both of us.

I realised then that September seemed to follow us both like a black dog. He used to say, 'September, always bloody September.'

I wrote, 'I can run now, Bob. So can you. I've undone the ties which bound me for so long.'

My last encounter with Bob, dark as it was, revealed an insight into myself and my years of co-dependence which stifled my growth; Bob had taken advantage of that stifling. 'I hope the blight of September is finally done and dusted. Goodbye, Bob. Fly away,' I wrote.

The Afterlife

Bob had drifted away slowly towards where the old church people of his youth, heaven, angels, parents and enemies were assembled waiting for him.

After the events at the mineshaft which ended his and his lost brother's life, John had raced on ahead, glancing back at the man who he thought was his friend and had ended his life. Pangs of pity flooded into his soul causing him to reach back to Bob. 'Come, mate, come. It's our journey.'

Bob looked back and shook his head, unable to come to terms with the early death of his brother and shocked that he had survived death itself.

John looked up and followed the light because his studies told him it would happen.

Bob sat muttering the last words he had spoken to John. 'No. No, not now. Not yet, maybe sooner or maybe later, John.' He hoped John on his new journey heard him.

John had reached his apogee in a blinding flash of light and was at the gates being welcomed. He hoped Bob would join them but Bob was stuck. He thought about Sunday school and the fascinating Bible tales yet he looked back to earth and saw people running about like ants escaping the rain. He saw a familiar church. A priest was speaking and mentioned Bob Allen. Mavis and Lorraine were sitting in the front row wearing dark glasses. He felt free to move and wished he was back in the old house and, whisk, in a flash he was back in the bathroom splashing on his Bay Rum and gazing in the mirror. Mavis was asleep but he had to wake her. She needed to know that he still survived death as she said he would on many occasions. An energy came upon him and he looked at their wedding photo in the lounge. The energy toppled the frame off its hook and it fell to the floor with a thud.

Mavis turned on the light and picked up the photo and a tear came into her eyes, which she wiped away, then she placed the frame back in place. She walked to the bathroom sniffing like a deer who has picked up a scent and he knew she had realised it was his Bay Rum. She looked around the room and shivered and then walked back to her bed. He followed her and soon she was in a dream. At least she thought she was, but somehow Bob had managed to worm into the dream and was alongside her in bed, whispering in her ear and making gentle love. The enjoyment of the earthly pleasure kept him close by for many months till the time he wanted her to come over to his plane and be with him. She rejected him at the last moment on the edge of the shaft and he knew he had lost her forever. He once again experienced a feeling of abandonment and ingratitude; after all, he had saved her from being violated by the giant in the north-west mining area camp.

She had found a new life and the green tinge of jealousy had risen within him when he saw the copper in her mobile home and they seemed to be getting on rather well; too well, he thought. He had to ask God for help but he didn't know how now that Mavis was a lost cause.

He found that time had no meaning in his present state, which was aided because of his work. He strove long and hard, admired his bricklaying and spoke endlessly to a God who did not reply, but he was insistent and kept it up.

'Am I getting closer to the gates, God?' And he was satisfied that God knew of his efforts and would one day reward him. Yet he became angry that his efforts were not rewarded and he thought about the Bible story of the Tower of Babel and saw that it was the way to reach God. 'Yes, that's it. I'll build a tower to find God.' He did not listen to the advice which was shouted down to him by the elders.

The people who had been in his life watched as the tower grew layer by layer and would call out, 'Come down, Bob. Come down, Bob. God is everywhere.'

John called out, as well as his mother, but his father was in another darker place.

At the end of each row, which lay straight, true and clean, he would stand in front of a full-length mirror which he had created and flexed his muscles and measured his arms with a tape. And smiled to himself in his self-adulation.

There came a time, after a few more rows were added, when he looked in the mirror. When he saw himself, he staggered and fell. The reflection he saw staring back at him was a man with thin arms, legs and small dainty hands. Warts and boils covered every part of his body, skin flaking off in large pieces.

A blinding overpowering thought came into his soul and he knew that each blemish was tangible evidence of all the people he had mistreated. In that instant, he watched as the tower crumbled and its broken bricks lay scattered about. Voices spoke, sounding like wind blowing through the gaps in the crumbled mortar.

'Stand, Bob, stand. It's done. Come, come with us, Bob.'

He walked on to the elders' council and sat at their table while they outlined his next adventure back on earth.

Five Years Later: Darwin, Northern Territory

The five-year-old boy with the unusually large hands was lost in his world of creativity in the sandpit containing many bricks which his elderly doting father had made for him. His parents Lorraine and Phillip Morton were away for the day and the boy was in the care of his grandmother Mavis Stock.

Michael Morton's birth was a surprise to his mother, who had long given up on the idea of another child. After all, she had stepchildren, some grown up long ago, and her own daughters. But the family loved Michael. His father Phillip was much older than his wife yet in very good health. He doted on the boy, which was strange considering he was a twenty-five-year regular army man with two tours under his belt in Vietnam. He had come home unscathed.

Mavis studied her watch a few times, expecting Michael's parents to arrive soon, along with her husband. Ken and she were raring to take the mobile home on a trip to Adelaide and then back across the Nullarbor to Darwin for three months. The van was already packed and seemed to say, 'Let's get going.'

She gazed at Michael's features and saw a part of Bob Allen in the child, at the same time hoping his ego would not expand and cause the problems Bob had. Her daughter agreed, but his father was overindulgent and would hear no talk of the child inheriting the obsessions of his long-dead grandfather.

'Come on now, Michael. Time to clean up. Mum and Dad will be home soon.'

Michael did not look up but said in a loud gruff voice, 'Piss off, Mavis.'

Those words brought back bitter memories for Mavis. She was

stumped for a reply and chose within seconds to say nothing. She just took his hand and walked with him to the bathroom. She ran a bath and turned round when she heard a noise. The boy had adjusted the full-length mirror and was posing with his arms curled up, revealing an unusually large muscle on his biceps.

She became angry and shouted out, 'Get here now, Michael.'

He sauntered over, obeying her words. Within seconds he had become the nice little boy he usually was.

She said a prayer. 'God, make him go away.' The words of her friend Sue about possession came back. She made a note to ring Sue as they would be in Adelaide within a month.

Mavis

We reached Adelaide sooner than I thought. The trip was uneventful. We stopped at van parks on the way down, taking turns to drive two hours each so we didn't have to deal with fatigue. Ken had attended many accident scenes as a uniform cop and a volunteer ambulance driver and I was always a careful driver so we both had the smarts in that area.

I had lived in a granny flat at Lorraine's house for a while before we decided to tie the knot.

Our marriage ceremony was held in a quiet Darwin park. Our extended family gathered. Lorraine held her two-year-old toddler, who kept reaching his arms out towards me, grabbing at me with large hands like Bob's, but I brushed out of my mind the thought of him turning out like his grandfather. I had given up the truck-driving job but some of my mates from there were in attendance.

Ken was an attentive husband. Since our marriage he never pestered me for sex but seemed to guess my mood and it was then a spontaneous magic moment. No snoring afterwards and we would talk or read into the wee small hours. As we had been on our own for a while, we were aware of the follies of being under one another's heels and hoped it would not happen.

Silently, though, we both thought being together in close quarters for three months might be an issue. However, we tried to work through it. Ken restored old furniture rather than be under my heels all day. Between yoga, my spiritualist group and cooking experiments I was busy, as well as looking after Michael from time to time. We took short fishing and walking trips on the weekends, which were relaxing and fun. Ken was an excellent bushie and knew all the tricks. I was in safe hands. He had many Aboriginal friends and he treated them with dignity which was returned in spades. However, we knew it wouldn't be Utopia all the time; nothing is – things go wrong and that's life.

Sue came to our wedding and became popular with guests as she was widely known as a great clairvoyant. She picked up many readings but I detected a bit of negativity within Ken – after all, he had been a pragmatic no-nonsense cop.

She spoke about young Michael and felt that he had inherited a strong part of Bob's genes and that it was possible he was reincarnated in his grandson, which she said was more common than not. Her talks with the spirit world always revealed that Bob's spirit had passed on, and she did not think it was a possession. I agreed with her. Ken did not comment. Her final suggestion was to keep an eye on Michael to ensure Bob's traits did not come out too often. However, how did I tell Lorraine? It was a puzzle.

I sensed Ken's uneasiness when Sue and I got down to talking about spirit and I gave him an out. 'Look, love, I know you think this all bullshit. Feel free to go for a walk if you like. See you in about an hour, OK?'

He nodded and walked out checking his watch.

'Now, Sue, you were saying about twin souls, right?'

'Yes, a guide came through in my last meet. His name was Freddie.'

'Do go on.'

'"We all have twin souls," he said in a deep mellow voice. "One stays in the afterlife as a guide while the other lives on the earth. It is a parallel life and we receive glimpses of it here on earth, maybe a shadow flicks and calls to us, and in our dreams it seems like *déjà vu.*"'

I was intrigued but chose not to interrupt.

She went on. 'Let's say you're in a coma or a drug-induced state. Your twin soul takes over and cares for you – actually occupies your body, giving you silent healing. And everyone who visits you when you're well says, "You've seen the light."'

'So we're both like passing ships in the night, then?'

'That's right, Mavis.'

'So what do we become over the years in the afterlife?'

'We emerge into a ball of healing light with part of our soul attached.'

'My God, that's unbelievable. I won't tell Ken, though. Funny, you know, he's seen the ghosts of some of his dead mates from Vietnam, but he has a struggle with the afterlife.'

'That's common. People usually sit on the fence until they gasp their last moments.'

'Dreams. I've been having a recurring dream. I wake up to the sound of squealing brakes. What do you think it means?'

'Without any more info, I wouldn't know. Maybe someone in a car nearby woke you up. Not everything is a message, Mavis.'

'I guess so.' My mind lingered for a while and I was in a type of automatic pilot for a few seconds.

Ken walked back, we had a meal and some fine white wines and set the alarm for six a.m. He was a punctual man and our next stop was Port Wakefield, then along the way to Port Augusta.

We passed through Port Augusta and made our way through the ranges towards Kimba, stopping at the Giant Galah statue for a time. Then it was off with a few more stops till we came to Ceduna for the night.

'Am I getting old, Ken?'

'Not as old as me, mate. I've got ten years up on you. I'm the one that's old. Why do you ask, white man?'

He was always cracking jokes so I followed up. 'Tell me, Tonto, what's the name of that great Aussie movie with Julia Blake and Leo McKern where they get together and drive to north Queensland in a Kombi? They get on one another's nerves not being used to each other.'

'Let me go through the alphabet. I might get it.'

'He dies eventually.'

Ken slipped a few words which did not make sense. 'Yep. Yep. Yep. Nearly there. Why do you ask, grasshopper?'

'O master. It mirrors my life.'

And we both burst out laughing.

'Let pain make you free, grasshopper.'

Ken contained himself but I knew he was deep in thought about it.

I broke the long silence. 'Look, Ken, as long as we can laugh we'll be good.'

Ken looked at me. 'I've pondered on this too 'cos that movie stuck with me. They were without any company apart from the neighbour. All we have to do on this trip is pull up at van parks. We'll soon meet other like-folk all the way to Kalbari. Lots of good sights through the south-west and great parks. Let's get out and see everything. OK, hon?'

His reassurance gave a positive spin to my rambling thoughts, and of course we could chat each night on the phone to our loved ones.

Love was there, we just had to make adjustments, and on this trip I discovered that Ken was touchy and unwilling to enter into dialogue if he felt he wasn't in control. The root causes weren't hard to define because he had a military career and a long police career which would have left him with an iron will. However, I had an iron will too because of my endurance and my change of career late in life. Not many women who had been in my position would have risked it. I took the ball and ran with it. So, in spite of the little titbits which come in the night, I reckoned I'd done well with this marriage.

We changed over as drivers quite a few times on the Nullarbor Plain after yawning, rolling eyes, making grunting noises and straightening up from our seated positions. On one occasion, Ken was unable to find a tree to relieve himself so he turned his back to the wind. A car full of rowdy teenagers slowed down and yelled, gesturing at Ken, who turned round and stuck his fingers up in the air, at the same time losing the grip on his trousers. He was still urinating and the wind blew the stream onto his beloved moleskins and into his desert boots.

I couldn't control my mirth and fell against the side of the van holding my stomach while he lurched back, legs apart and resembling an exhausted marathon runner who had run the distance with broken shoelaces. I calmed down and started to goad him, studying the spreading wet patch.

I said, 'How am I going to get the creases back into those now?'

He stared at me bleakly and I thought, 'Whoops.'

He became sullen and I could see his anger rising, yet I was still amused. His eyes were flashing and his lips were pursed ready to give me a burst, which was rare. He opened his mouth and took a breath and then suddenly his top false teeth fell down. He tried to yell out 'Shit' but nothing came out.

It was too much for me. I laughed out loud and slapped the top of the door jamb, which bruised my finger, and I yelled out loud, 'Bastard.'

His expression changed in an instant from a grin to a laugh when he saw my discomfort. He shook his head and I realised my old Ken was back, because he was a man of much altruism.

We settled down and apart from some greasy marks on the rear-vision mirror and the loud music he was playing, we started to enjoy the sights as we drive off the great plain.

An hour had gone by when Ken casually said, 'Don't look now but there's a red Indian sitting in the back.'

I still couldn't help myself and milked his words as best as I could and I must have had a twinkle in my eye when I spoke.   'White man speak with forked tongue.'

But he was serious. His eyes were closed. 'He's sending a message to me saying something about a Spanish dancer.'

Glibly I replied, 'Perhaps you'll get lucky.'

Wrong again. His sullen expression returned but I saw that he was sound asleep, and had been all along. I was intrigued and wondered if he had a red Indian spirit guide who sent him a puzzling or maybe cryptic message.

We stopped at van parks as Ken suggested and had a lot of company, being surrounded by interesting grey nomads who spent their lives on the road in between picking fruit for a few bucks to pay for the diesel. There was no more talk of Spanish dancers and I was able to wash and iron his moleskins at Albany.

Ken had a personal victory when he handed the beloved trousers over to me. His eyes shone when he spoke. 'The only creases we should worry about are those in our brains.' He had finally outwitted me (for the moment, I thought).

We were close to Darwin and, apart from a few small hiccups when our brains were out of kilter with each other, the sights we had seen and the fun we had made the trip rewarding. But we vowed never to make a trip that long again. We are family- and home-loving folk. Ken had missed his woodwork and I my yoga and my group and I was looking forward to it and said so.

Ken looked at me with a bit of a sneer and said, 'You're like a bunch of witches.'

I braked suddenly and moved over to the edge of the road and jumped out. He followed and I could see he felt sorry for his silly remarks.

I looked him full in the face, which was difficult because of his height, and folded my arms across my chest. I was angry yet calm. 'Don't knock what you know nothing about. This is the last time, Ken. Do you read me?' I enunciated the last few words with pauses.

He swallowed, his Adam's apple moving up and down like a stationary steam train's engine throbbing away at the railway terminus. He gulped and turned his face away from me and I'm of the opinion that at that point he was scared of me and my spirit group.

'OK. So it's a sisterhood with blood ties, I gather. I'm open. Tell me about it.'

I did. It was a long narrative but he listened without any interruption.

'It started round 1646 in the UK. It was the time of the witchfinder Matthew Hopkins and people were betraying neighbours for the money and the property which they might inherit after the so-called witches were hanged. It seems that a noble lady, a widow, quite young, married a commoner who was shagging around, unknown to her. He denounced her, claiming he had seen her dance naked with other women around a fire in the forest. Classic stuff, really. Hopkins needed a hit on a woman of power and offered a bag of gold to the husband, who quickly made up the good yarn. She was tried and led to the gallows. Her last words were thrown at Hopkins and the husband, in the crowd with his new love, crying crocodile tears. '"I curse the Lord of my lands now. The seventh son in each generation will die a miserable death." She died in a bout of strangulation and Hopkins apparently wanked in the bush later. The curse continued. The denouncer had six children who were all mentally challenged. His seventh son drowned in a lake at age three years. The new wife died giving birth to the boy and the father hanged himself in an act of contrition.'

Ken said, 'What a payback. There's more, I suppose?'

'Yep. Down through the centuries, all the wives of the Walkers, Taylors, Hughes and a few others always protect their men. Most of them appreciate the nurturing, though I can't say that my ex did much in that direction, though it was part of the controlling nature of his male forebears.'

'Curses work if you believe them, mate. I've seen it happen with our Aboriginals.'

I smirked. 'Ya reckon, do you? I think differently. Once they're locked in on the airwaves, they act like energy, and energy can't be destroyed.'

'So what happens at your group? Is there a leader?'

'Of course, but I'm compelled to keep that a secret.'

'Do you cast spells or stuff like that?'

I flushed at the tenor of his question and hostility flared. 'Bloody hell, Ken, what do you think we are? We're not a force of evil. We're more like a group of ladies who give good advice on how to help with marriage problems. There's a bloody lot of written material in our hands. It's survived for many years and it's still good. No, I'm not about to tell you what the advice is.'

He stroked his chin and looked out the car window, framing an answer. He spoke to the wind. 'I'm not complaining, love. It's clear to me now that it is a force of good.'

I stopped for a while and looked at him and saw the thoughtful expression as he sat with his arms folded. His lips moved without words as if he was putting together evidence. We alighted from the car and walked around hand in hand, kicking small stones. I looked up in the sky and saw a huge black cloud which danced sideways. It was otherwise a clear sky and the back of my head itched as it always did when bad news came my way. Yet I said nothing about it to Ken.

Ken never uttered another word which I might consider as sarcastic about my beliefs. I was overjoyed to be home again, as was Ken, and our lives returned to the state they were in before our minor mishaps on the journey.

Ken drove down to the army reunion held each year at Katherine, where I suspect gallons of beer, black slapping, rough talk and careful talk about absent comrades occupied the entire five days, because he came back bleary-eyed and with his favourite moleskins filthy.

There was a different look on his features when he spoke. 'Love, on the way back I called in to the army medics at Darwin for a check-up and some tests. I've been having some complications with my bowels. It started on the trip.' He paused.

The enormity of his words struck me like a brick thrown at my head. I rushed into his open arms and started to sob.

He stroked my head in the gentle way he always did with his long piano player's fingers and lifted my chin. His eyes were full of tears. Yet he was able to speak. 'It's full-on bowel cancer.'

I pushed him away with my left arm and could not look without blinking at his face with the deep hazel eyes. I looked down and then I fell sobbing on the carpet. He walked away realising he could do nothing at this point and went outside into his shed. I heard the sound of the planer grumbling away. So I put the kettle on and made his favourite cup of coffee, milk and two. I wiped my tears and stood straight. Ken needed me now, not a wreck, not a victim; he needed my strength. 'Help me, God,' I said as I walked out to the shed, but the coffee was spilt by my shaking hands when I reached the shed.

'No matter, love, no matter,' he said. He opened his bar fridge and poured out two glasses of Margaret River Chardonnay and we sat on the chairs.

He held my hand and spoke again. 'Twelve months.'

I nodded obliquely and thought about the Spanish dancer. The guide was trying to tell him he had cancer, which rhymes with Spanish dancer. And there he was on the trip cracking jokes and with me trying to match him in one-upmanship. So much for my journey to find myself and to cope on my own. My God, how would I cope now?

Ken maintained his stoic self right till the end. It was twelve months as predicted. He underwent the colonostomies, the radiation, when he lost his full head of ash-grey wavy hair, the chemo and other intrusions into his body until it spread to the bones. He needed a mobile chair but he still cracked jokes.

I was with him at the end when the sound of the machine played its one note.

He opened his eyes and called out, 'Dad, Dad,' and I'm sure he saw his father at the end. We should be careful what we wish for or what we pray for.

It was appropriate in my case and I had feelings of regret which will never leave me. I wished for some distance on the trip and I sure got it – permanently. Now he was gone I'd get on with my life but he wasn't here to share it with me. I felt a void, an aching empty feeling. I wept for my loss. I hoped in time to pray to God with gratitude but at the moment it was too hard.

Another unsung hero had passed on and I was for a time bereft of any tears. But the dreams came on, as did my spirit group, where I received many messages from Ken that he was well. He once came through and said, 'Don't drive the van again.' I decided I would either sell it or donate it to charity as a mobile soup kitchen.

The dream of squealing brakes came back a few months after I lost my great love. And then it either faded away or I did not remember it when I woke up each day.

Fifteen Years Later

Mavis filled her life and it became a joy to watch the family grow. Michael had his eyes set on a legal career and passed with high marks at the university in Perth and was headed for a career with the West Australian Department of Public Prosecutions. Michael's controlling traits were not obvious, though Mavis's friend Sue thought otherwise. His mother dismissed any talk of the genes coming through to her son. Mavis donated the mobile home to a family trust after her extended family wanted to keep it in the family. She was happy to see the last of it because she never took another step into it after the message came through from Ken. Her stepchildren were settled into motherhood and one lived in London.

She heard that Judy Downley had returned from living in Thailand because of her daughter's urgings and recurring bouts of malaria. They lived on a large property in north Queensland where Judy grew herbs and made potions which cured many people.

Mavis lived in Ken's house, which she had inherited in the will, and ensured that it would not change. All the family would inherit the house after she passed. She maintained good health and walked rather than drive her small car. Her volunteer work with disabled people was widely known. She would visit and offer good books which she bought in bulk and would provide comfort in a small way. She often read short chapters to them.

Mavis woke up with a start. The dream had returned. It was the sound of squealing brakes. She made a note to ring her friend in Adelaide, hoping for an answer to the puzzle.

She walked out onto the street at six a.m.. It was a brisk morning which caused her to warm up with her stretches and twists.

The garbage man drove past, waved and called out, 'G'day, Mavis.'

She waved back. A quick glance to the left and the right and, dressed in her best tracksuit and wearing her Puma joggers, she stepped onto the road.

A sound flashed sharply in to her memory – the sound of squealing brakes. Her dream. She never saw the light-coloured car because of the bright sun and the fact that it was travelling at high speed in the hands of a drunken driver. It struck her on the right side of her body. Her ribs instantly cracked, and the gay-coloured parrots which she always fed flew away into the sky. The impact flung her high into the air. She landed on her face on the road and lay still and her breath slipped out – along with the blood and brain matter.

Her seventieth birthday had just passed on the fresh September morning.

The neighbours ran out wringing their hands and yelling, 'Get an ambulance,' and the sound of sirens was soon heard.

Epilogue: Five Days Later

The crowd gathered at the service in a funeral home in Darwin. A cremation and a scattering of ashes had been ordered some time before by the deceased. There was no formal religious service, but rather a few words with appropriate speakers addressing the huge crowd of mourners.

The chairperson of her spiritual group spoke kind and generous words about her friend, as did Sue, who had flown from Adelaide to honour her old friend.

Her grandson Michael spoke with some elegance; he had flown in from Perth after having been accepted as a lawyer with the WA DPP. The love he felt for his grandmother was obvious because his voice cracked a few times. He spoke of the tragedies which she and the family had witnessed. His father Phillip dying years ago and later Ken Stock, Pop, as he called him, and Mavis's beloved husband. Her grief which was tangible for many years yet she endured and then to be struck down a few days after her birthday. He hoped it had been quick and that she did not suffer.

Lorraine came last. She stood straight like her mother said she should at the lectern. A widow (twice) talking to another widow (twice) now passed. She cleared her throat and began to speak, softly at first with timely gaps, and the audience sat still, no movement, no scratching sounds, no coughs; some held back tears. There was a fluttering of tissues from the crowd being crunched in the hands of still, silent people.

'Before the black and white check bands massed outside her front window. Before the gavel banged with its sharp sound fracturing the emotion-charged atmosphere of the courtroom, before the magistrate pronounced his careful words, Mavis Allen was just an ordinary housewife with an abusive husband, a daughter and two grandchildren living in middle-class Australia. Within the space of a few years, her life would be shaken and stirred.'

No one moved for the rest of her speech, no feet shuffled. Lorraine had captured the moment, as she intended.

Time stood still in the parlour on that wet Darwin day during the month of September.

Shalom, Samuel

'I shall not commit the fashionable stupidity of regarding everything I cannot explain as a fraud.' – Carl Jung

Prologue

The Kent Town Salvation Army Boys' Home on Portrush Road in Adelaide's fashionable eastern suburbs was a giant old colonial mansion donated by a grateful citizen many years ago. Some residents remarked that it look sinister, though nothing untoward had been reported. Maybe it had a look about it, a look of old South Carolina with its giant deciduous trees breaking the skyline, or maybe it was just the wind which continuously blew across the trees. It was a haven to possums, whose bright shiny eyes stared down on the passing parade of young people dashing home in the night after watching an old Boris Karloff movie, their hurried footsteps rapidly sinking away into the night.

The home was bursting at the sides with the influx of boys in 1943. The children were orphans, the rarely thought of victims whose parents were either away at war, dead or incapacitated or, worse, had deserted in droves to follow their own lives without compassion for the children left abandoned.

A five-year-old boy sat on a frosty cement seat just inside the entrance to the mansion, his feet barely touching the damp five a.m. grass. A sharp gully wind blew from the east, piling the leaves under his feet.

The child picked up one of the leaves and smelt it, fondling it, and for some unknown reason placed the leaf in the pocket of his oversized grey jacket done up to the neck.

He grimaced with the pain of his toenails inside wet socks encased by sandals with broken straps. His socks concealed the bloodstains of dried scabs from a botched attempt some hours before to cut his toenails, which had exposed the quicks.

The rough, rectangular asbestos placard secured by old rusty wire around his neck irritated the boy. He choked and coughed up saliva in trying to remove the placard, which had in capital letters the words 'ORPHAN…PARENTS DEAD…MOTHER OF A LUNG DISEASE AND FATHER KILLED AT TOBRUK IN 1941'. There were other papers inside the pockets of the grey coat which revealed some pieces of information such as the time, date and place where he was born.

Samuel didn't hear the clanking sound of pint bottles of milk, with cream under the stopper, being delivered by Fred the milkman in his horse-drawn cart onto the front doorstep of each house or into a wooden box near the front gate. If he had, he would have jumped up, however painfully, to pat the old horse like his mother did before she had got sick. He just remembered the smell of her bad breath when she used to trip over and spill the bottle on his pyjamas.

Fred saw a man in his mid-twenties wearing an army greatcoat with two stripes on the sleeves jumping back onto an idling motorcycle and sidecar. Fred recognised the uniform as the man made a U-turn and travelled north along Portrush Road. He gave no more thought to the man because it was common of late to see soldiers riding around on motorcycles. Yet within seconds he was shocked by the sight of the freezing small boy sitting on the concrete seat inside the gate of the old home, which was at the end of his round and where he delivered many bottles for the orphans.

His old horse stopped, enjoying the feedbag which Fred, expecting to be absent for a time, hung round its neck. Fred picked up the poor freezing child and carrying him to the front door.

The porch light went on. Allan Parsons, his World War I friend from the RSL, sized up the situation and plucked the child from the arms of the milkman.

'On the bloody steps, do you mind, Allan! Jesus, some people.'

Allan nodded and at the same time pressed the Nurse button. 'Did you see who dumped him, mate?'

'No, but he was wearing a uniform with corporal's stripes. U-turned past me and drove off on a Panther and sidecar. I've got one, so I know. Didn't get the number, though… Sorry, mate.'

'Yeah, I had one of those. Slopy Panther. Long stroke. Fires between each stobie pole, so they say.' And he added a few more words to the milkman's concerns. 'Thanks, mate. We'll look after him. Had a few more like this this week.'

Allan sat the child on the hall table. It was then that he saw the sallow complexion and the aquiline nose with the black eyes. Jewish children were rare in the eastern suburbs. The Star of David gleamed with its glittering gold dangling around the boy's neck.

The attendants were busy removing his wet socks when Samuel dug deep into the grey pockets of the coat and pulled out an adult-size harmonica. And a wet autumn tree leaf as well.

He placed the instrument to his blue lips and started to play, and out came a perfect rendition of 'Waltzing Matilda'. At the end of the perfect notes, the child climbed off the table and started to do a little tap dance on the old slate floor. He bowed at the end of the tune.

They clapped him silently, not wishing to wake the other sleeping boys.

'Joan, we are in the presence of a genius, I believe.'

Joan was crying at this point and could not find words to answer Allan.

They shuffled through his papers and saw his name: Samuel Jacob Samuels. The birth certificate revealed a clumsy attempt to scrub out the name of the father. Someone loved the boy at some distant point in his short life because written in a gentle hand with loops and whirls were the two words 'Shalom, Samuel'.

The institution, after a short conference, vowed not to reveal that the boy was Jewish until he was eighteen years of age. Not out of bigotry but rather to give him a more pleasant journey in a new chapter of his life.

1

Sergeant Joe Bedford

Balikpapan, Borneo, July 1945

I sat with him on the hot beach sands after the landing and watched the flickering flames soaring up into the red sky, a sky red with the oil fires from large storage tanks blazing for days. There he was among half of the battalion. My guess is maybe six hundred dead of our soldiers lay strewn about and my corporal mate, Harry Jacobs Samuels, was close to death as I watched the blood bubbling from evenly spaced holes in his chest. They had been delivered by a twenty-five-calibre 'woodpecker' Jap machine gun. Aptly named, we thought, though most of us had never seen one of the birds which gave it its name.

We had been together since 1942 in the 7th Division, me a sergeant and him a corporal later on. Harry was an honourable man. Never minded about the slings of 'Jew boy'. He could give back a few quips himself.

All of that aside, when we had bad moments he would entertain us with his mouth organ and do a tap dance, which broke the fear or whatever, and brought about cheers, tears and laughter. A real bloody character. Like all of us, a Depression kid; and a great pilferer. Before he joined up, he used a few different names mainly to avoid the cops because of his occasional stealing Violet Crumble bars from a shop or knocking off a few tools here and there to make a few bob.

We heard that the family had money, being good Jews in Melbourne, but he never spoke much about it. His older brother Aaron was killed at Tobruk in 1941.

Harry had a nephew named Samuel and I didn't realise until the night before we hit the beach the depth of shame he felt after he'd been dumped with the Salvos in 1943.

But there was a hell of a lot more which came out last night. My silent mouth and eyes must have been as wide as saucers when the engrossing tales poured out of his mouth.

He had fears about the landing and dreams of death. Atonement was on his mind and occupied us all that sleepless night. We started swapping all sorts of secrets yet he asked me straight out – staring at me with his big black eyes and wiping snot from his big nose with the back of his blackened big hands, but hands which could also tickle a violin's strings; I know, because I heard him play a few times – 'Do you believe in ghosts?'

I looked at him, searching for any answer which might end the scary subject, but nothing came out.

'My mother came to me after she died, when I was about nine years old. She was standing at the foot of my bed facing the window. I still can see it now as the sun blazed through the open curtains…yet there was no shadow. She didn't turn right away and I was sitting up gaping at her, shading my eyes from the sunlight. I held my legs and heard the sound of my heart going thump thump thump thump, beating steady like the engines of this ship – that's what brought it all back to me. She turned and faced me. Her eyes were sad and forlorn and in that instant a sudden cloud from outside chased the phantom away. I called to her., 'Mum, Mum,' but she was gone in a blink.'

'Did she come back again, Harry?' I was fearful at this point.

'Yes. Two nights ago when the ship was crawling into the harbour, I stirred and saw her sitting on the edge of my bunk. She was smiling. She said, 'You must make amends, Harry. Do it soon.' I knew what she meant.'

I butted in when Harry stopped for a breath. I understood because my mother came back to me a couple of times recently with messages from beyond the grave. 'Yes, mate, so do I.'

And once again he looked into my eyes and spoke softly. 'I have a child called Samuel. I dumped him on a cold night at Kent Town.'

When he told me of his adultery with his brother's wife, I looked at him and the full impact flashed to me. The shame of it all flooded his features and this time his eyes were downcast. He scratched the ship's deck with his fingernails so hard that it drew blood, like he was trying to punish himself to prove to God that he was sorry.

A question begged to be asked. 'How? I mean, how did it happen? Rachel, is that her name?'

'Yes. Aaron was away doing his train job and I was in the next room. It was 1938. It happened only once, mind you, but she was pregnant as a result of our sin. Aaron came home and was joyous about a baby coming. I didn't stick around and started to get in some trouble with the cops so I pissed off, just wandering, cutting wood, panning for gold, knocking off stuff. Mainly food.'

'So in time Aaron found out, I suppose.'

'Yes. I reckon Samuel would have been about one. There must have been a huge argument because Aaron joined the army in 1939. The rest is history. He came back on leave with broken ribs and was killed in 1941 at Tobruk.'

I made no judgement of Harry right then. After all, there was a good chance we would all be killed on the landing. 'Mother of God, what a story! Bloody biblical really.'

I thought about all the kings of the Hebrews, Moses, David and Bathsheba (I too know my Bible) and a hell of a lot of other stuff. There was clearly more on Harry's mind, so I asked what it was.

'Mum came to me for a reason… I'm not going to make it. That I know. I can almost smell my death. I've filled out a will for Samuel for his eighteenth birthday. He's to get a thousand pounds which I've saved in the Commonwealth Bank. When he's twenty-one, he'll inherit a house in St Kilda left to me a year ago by a wealthy old aunt. I was her favourite. I put papers about his birth in his pocket when I dumped him, and a harmonica, which I taught him to play when I boarded at Rachel's house for a while again after Aaron was killed. But no funny business this time. Samuel must have been totally confused with the comings and goings of two soldiers in uniform. Rachel's sad drift into melancholy and her neglect of the boy caused the home to finally collapse. I was forced to take him away and was stuck with what to do. I was called back to the army and didn't want him to be a ward of the state. She died while I watched. And her last gasps were pitiful… I could hardly watch. I had to avert my eyes. I gathered Samuel up and took him to the Salvos. At least, I thought, he'd get a reasonable life. But it's caused me untold problems since that day. God will punish me for this, you know, Joe.'

'Dunno about punishment, mate. If this kid has inherited your gifts, he could make it.'

Harry thought on this and his face lit up as red as a baboon's bum, clouding over his normally dark, sallow complexion. 'Yes, and he can tap dance. He's going places, that kid of mine.'

'How did the dancing happen?'

'Before she got sick, she took him to Lorna Badman's dance class at Norwood. You see, Rachel was a dancer as well. What a shame. What a bloody shame.'

'So are you going to let him know at some point who his father is?'

'Not yet. Too cowardly. He's got to grow first.'

'How do you expect he'll find out the secret?'

'See this bottle?' He produced a glass bottle with a stopper. 'I'm slipping the secret into canvas…along with another Shalom message. Maybe one day when he's mature it will lob his way. With God's help, I hope.'

'Do you want me to witness it?'

'Yes, and sign it, and then chuck it overboard, please.'

Which I did and heard the splash and watched the bottle bobbing away from the ship while the tide took it out to sea.

I had one last question. 'If the bottle doesn't make it, it have you got a backup plan?'

He nodded. 'The Melbourne lawyers will let him know. I pray he'll have a good life and not have to fight a war.'

We drank a bottle of brandy between us that night and woke early with a start from the sound of our bugles. We loaded our webbing and checked our rifles and prepared to disembark from the ship.

2

Balikpapan, Borneo, July 1945

Harry looked down at his body, legs twisted in an unnatural shape, and watched as the Japanese officer ran towards Joe with a sword raised. He wished he could yell and warn his friend but nothing came out.

Joe turned at the last moment and stuck his bayonet straight into the stomach of the short soldier, throwing the man into the air still pinioned on the great bayonet. The screaming man fell off and Harry watched while savagery took hold of Joe (and there was a savage in all of them). Joe thrust his bayonet time and time again into the dead soldier until his intestines fell out.

'Enough, enough, Joe.'

But Joe could not hear the words from his dead friend's spirit.

In that silent second a stillness came across Harry and he watched as Joe reached in the pockets of the soldier and drew out a photo of a family and three children.

Joe sat, rather fell, on his haunches, not caring about a war of rushing dying men. He wrapped his hands around his knees and rocked back and forth making no sounds. His Balikpapan war was over for a short time.

Harry felt a strong surge to move on, not upwards but to just move on. A strange heat came over him when he settled into a walk with his feet brushing an incandescent surface filled with small animals and bright coloured birds. People walked towards him. He recognised long passed-over relatives who without sound came up to him and took his hand.

Harry did not look back because he knew all would be well with Joe and the bottle would be found one day.

A new chapter for Harry had dawned.

3

Adelaide

1940

Samuel bounced about in his cot restless and uncomfortable with his unchanged nappy and the rash which came with it. The Johnson's baby powder chucked down the front of his groin did not help; when it was dry it merely stuck to his tender groin. The circumcision which occurred after his birth was also raw and scabs formed and fell off. He heard his mother's scream echoing again in the next room, in the small damp flat tucked away in a small street within the western suburbs of Adelaide.

Then there was the man in the smelly rough clothes and bandages who stood and glared at him, which made the child close his eyes and look away.

'No, no. Aaron, please' were the words spoken but they just sounded like a blur to him, unimaginable, which made him once again cry until the bottle with the milk was shoved roughly into his mouth, and for a few minutes he was lost in the sucking sound of the milk which he liked.

Back she would come again with her face bending down into his – silent, mouthing words which did not come out – and then snatching away the bottle, holding her nose and walking away while he lay in his mess.

A clean-smelling lady came in later and picked him up, then carried him outside, where she changed his nappy under the gaze of his mother.

'We'll take this child away from you. You do understand, don't you?'

And his mother, who now cuddled him in her arms, kept repeating, 'Sorry. Sorry. Sorry.'

Samuel knew those words and said them in his sleep.

Yet her screams did not stop, they grew louder, and he found a way to stop them by blocking his ears with his hands.

He could not make out the man's words, loud though his voice was. 'Bitch, bitch. My bloody brother. How could you, how could you?'

She sobbed so loud that the residents in the adjacent flat banged on the door.

More voices said, 'Keep it down or I'll call the cops.'

Then she cried silently and the man still yelled.

'He's not mine…just a bastard from bloody Harry… God help me. God help me.'

The man came into his room and Saumel knew he was there and closed his eyes. But the word 'bastard' stayed within his cells and it was repeated once again. 'A bastard born of adultery.'

Samuel was familiar with the sound of a door slamming. Once again he heard it slam and the man with the smelly clothes and the white bandages left the room .It was quiet once again. And Samuel gurgled again.

1941

Samuel had a birthday; he even had a cake. His mother smelled better and his bed was nice and he had an uncle who stayed at the house. Samuel liked him; he was better than the other man, who always glared at him.

Sometimes during the night he thought the angry man sat on his bed crying. 'Mum, that man who shouted at you sits on my bed and cries.'

He watched the looks between his uncle and his mother, their eyes opening and closing, and he heard them say, 'He hated Samuel. Called him a bastard.'

But his uncle said nothing. He loved the mouth organ which the man had given him and they both played tunes on the instrument. It was his best time then.

December 1942

His mum would dance with his Uncle Harry and then one day they took him to a place on a tram and walked to what he thought they said was a dance school. The lady came out and Samuel looked at her, smelled her perfume and her nice dress with the beads, which he fondled.

'OK, Rachael. Show me what he can do.'

And Samuel tap danced to the applause of the lady with the beads.

'Bring him back. He has a future.'

His mum spoke. 'He can play the mouth organ as well – at the same time.'

Samuel loved people clapping him and after he had finished they came over and patted him and gave him a Violet Crumble bar which he munched all the way back in the tram.

May 1943

There came a time when she was sick again. She smelled again like the dog next door and Samuel cried again till two ladies with white clothes took them both to a big place with other people in white clothes.

He stayed with them in a special bed until his Uncle Harry came and sat down at his bed. Harry cried and the two ladies cried when they took him to her room. His mother looked nice and smelled better but she took him in her arms and hugged him just as he felt her arms flopping. He looked at her and saw her eyes close.

'Come, Samuel. Come back with me. Your mother's now in heaven.'

But he had no idea what heaven was, though he had seen dead cats on the road and knew they were in another place. As was his mother now.

During the night he woke up and saw her again in the bed with him and knew she was not dead. He turned over and slept. When he woke up in the morning he reached out to touch her and saw she was not there any more and Uncle Harry, who sat in the chair all night, once again said, 'She's in heaven now, Samuel.'

They took out their instruments and played a tune. Harry did a dance and Samuel watched.

Harry spoke. 'Cry now, Samuel. Cry.'

But Samuel could not cry; there were no more tears left in the five-year-old boy.

Winter 1943

Samuel sat on the cold steps inside the gate at the big house and heard the motorbike's noise as it drove away in the distance.

The smell of his uncle's big wet woollen coat faded away and he heard the clip-clop of the horse which stopped at the gate; the horse manure dropping on the road, with its sour smell and steam rising into the cold air; and the chomping of hay from the feedbag loosely tied around the horse's neck.

And the man who smelled of milk picked him up and rushed with him to the great doors of the old mansion.

4

Samuel

We dreamed a lot, us collection of abandoned boys. Groans and screams were followed by shouts from carers who yelled at the boys for wetting their beds. Some nights were pure chaos till we grew a bit and controlled our bladders – a bit.

Our dreams were possibly a collection of energies flying out to a marshalling area somewhere above our heads and returning again each night with the same old themes parked in amongst the fragmented individual experiences.

The reality of those dreams, jumbled up, was impossible to interpret for young boys so they waited for years till the spark of an incident rushed back to resurrect the past.

My beliefs about my dreams have never changed. They were the moments which started the music, the beginnings of my music career and my love of photography, which took me into the moment, which all came together as my compositions – later on, down the track.

It would not have happened without the winter of 1943. I am certain on that issue and believe my orphan life visited an inner strength within my being.

Are there any other pluses to being an orphan? There are no jealous siblings like a second child ready to steal your treasures, not that we had many in the big home. I was an exception; I had my harmonica, which I could play and entertain my friends with, and my friends were all I had.

The neglect I felt as a baby drove my soul to accept the joy of a warm bed, clean clothes and some belly-filling no-frills food. Us band of brothers stuck together as if a giant can of treacle entwined us all, and dotted in amongst the sticky sweet material was the imprint of our lives. We were able to dip our fingers in the metaphorical sweet link and suck from it much of our past, yet spitting out some and salivating on other portions.

Whispers punctuated the air regarding the downside of our lives which involved the overuse of the cane to keep us in line; not many of us were spared. Even the kids with polio and leg irons who clump-clumped away on their walk to the Norwood primary school were not spared, though, God bless them, they tried to stay in step, which isn't easy when some irons are shorter than others.

How a carer could beat one of those disabled kids was beyond my belief, which is a view I still hold.

I was compliant because it was much easier. Not a dobber, though. Just a keep-your-head-down sort of kid. I had other plans. The pecking order with the older boys had to be negotiated carefully lest you might find yourself getting a thrashing behind the outdoor toilets.

Puberty hit all of us around eleven years of age with the musty smells of wet dreams getting many of us into more trouble. But Allan Parsons saved me with his chats about the burgeoning problems of that stage of my life.

However, I was close to getting the 'cuts' one day from old Melon Head. His nickname, from his full name, Mr Fellenmein, was appropriate; he had a giant round head and thick glasses like the bottoms of milk bottles from which shone bulging eyes, dancing around from top to bottom and side to side whenever he was displeased, which was usually most of the day.

I did not like him nor he me. There were many reasons but one overriding reason was his treatment of the Aboriginal boys. They were natural athletes and perhaps he was jealous of their skills because I never saw him move very far from his chair or from standing behind us with the ogle in place – ever constant.

I'm sure his jealousy of my musical attributes was high on his list but what really upset him was when I interrupted him talking. It was just a sneeze and a cough, nothing more, yet he did not wait for my apology. Instead he yelled at me, 'Go into the next room and wait.'

I was just about to comply when he grabbed a piece of cardboard, scrawled on it, 'Full of cheek' and hung two pieces of wire on each end: he slung it around my neck.

My old memories of the placard long ago came back. I yanked the new one off and walked out, throwing it on the floor. The class murmured and were instantly dismissed from the room.

I knew I was in trouble when I heard the swishing of his cane just behind me.

'Drop your pants,' he whispered.

So I did, closing my eyes as well, waiting for the bite of the cane. Nothing happened. I saw out of the corner of my eye that he had squatted on the floor, uncomfortably for me due to his closeness.

I heard the sound of a zipper being pulled down and felt rough fat fingers touching, searching my behind. It was too much. I turned round to face a great stiff cock being pulled with his right hand. His eyes were closed behind the great glasses and then I smelt it, the sickly smell, but I did not look. I stood, pulled up my trousers and walked to the door.

He was on his feet by now with stains all down the front of his black pants. He blocked my exit with his arm. 'Don't tell or I'll get you one night outside.'

I ducked under his white hairless arms and walked out.

A year later old Melon Head tried his tricks in the Botanic Gardens public toilet. He was bashed and kicked so badly that he had a stroke. We rejoiced, happy to know he was not with us any more.

It was no surprise to me when I found out down the track that my younger friend Tom Watson had copped the full brunt of Melon Head's sexual antics.

My drive to succeed throughout my school years pushed me towards the Norwood high school at age twelve. The school opened a new chapter with the hobbies and creative pursuits it offered. I chose photography, which was a smart move for later in life when I dabbled between music and photo journalism. Sports such as swimming, soccer and the art of gymnastics took up any excess energy I had in those early teen years.

I won a music scholarship, assisted by my old friend Allan Parsons, and in no time I was sixteen years of age and had completed leaving honours.

Allan, the man of many connections, was able to get a job for me at a well known Rundle Street music store, which I loved. Money jangled in my pockets now and I was able to play my instruments (piano and mouth organ) to customers as well as advising them which long-playing records they might like to hear and purchase.

My favourite movie theatre was opposite. It was a small newsreel outlet called the Savoy. And I became obsessed with images of the Holocaust. The worst one was of a small four-year-old Jewish boy with a placard around his neck inscribed with the word 'JUDEN'. The horror of it all always left me in tears but I could not turn my eyes away from the little boy and those devils who called themselves the 'Master Race'.

For a time, the newsreels and my obsessive search for more horrors left me flat, so flat I could not concentrate on my studies, till Allan pulled me out of the mire. He concluded with some comforting phrases: 'You'll find a way, Samuel, to get over it. Trust me, I know.'

The unlocked secrets of my life were about to be revealed, which brought about a release from the horrors, and with that release came the knowledge of good fortune entering into my life.

My employers were of Jewish descent and, apart from my best guesses from overheard cupped-hand words, I knew in my heart that I was of their race. I just needed someone to tell me. Someone in the know or some paperwork. My bosses were kindly and invited me to eat with them at times and they must have felt constrained not to shout out from the rooftops but their friendship with Allan held back their words.

So there we were, all of my bosses, Allan and me circling around the subject but without anyone one prepared to open it up.

I bought a very good second-hand Super Elliot bike with all the ratchets, all the gears, mudguards, lights (battery-operated) and most of all a pump and puncture outfit. My bank book grew. However, I was not aware of a substantial sum which was soon to come. I was then seventeen and a half.

I knocked off one summer night after a stocktake and rode to the Torrens River. I took in the sounds of the birds, the lions and tigers barking and coughing in the zoo just behind, and monkeys gibbering, leaping from tree to tree. The night was humid and still and I stood right at the bank gazing at the still small river.

I heard the sound of running from behind and a thump thump sound on the grass. I did not look back yet I knew someone was going to attack me. I stuck out my right foot and heard a gasp as a heavy man tripped and splashed into the water. There he was, kicking and struggling, and I could see from his face that he could not swim.

Yet I walked away some distance. And then came a voice, a woman's voice. I smelt the lavender perfume right in my face and knew it was my mother.

'Go back, Samuel, go back. Help the man.' And the perfume just drifted into the mix of frangipani trees nearby.

I turned round and ambled back. Mother had gone.

'Lie on your back now,' I called sharply. And he did. 'Kick your legs.'

He blubbered, 'I can't swim.'

'Yes you can…do it.'

And he did, reaching the bank and clawing his way up from the tree roots nearby. He coughed and blubbered, 'Thanks, mate. I know now I can swim. I'm sorry I tried to hurt you.'

'OK,' I replied and then rode my bike to Norwood just as the boys were being lectured about doing a good deed each day.

Some said they had given a man an apple, helped an old lady across the road, picked up a banana skin in case someone tripped on it and so on.

I was asked, 'What did you do today, Samuel?'

I thought about it and said, 'I taught a man to swim.'

They clapped but I grinned to myself and recalled I had been in the process of letting him drown. Maybe a hardness had developed within me.

Mum came back that night and smiled at me in my dream but spoke no words.

5

Allan Parsons

The will and papers from the Melbourne lawyers had arrived so we waited till it was right to tell him. It seemed to me that it ought not to be dumped entirely in his lap on his eighteenth birthday. The board allowed me to be flexible. In any case, he could not inherit the properties until he was twenty-one and I guessed with the plans I had in mind for him that those matters were best carried out by the St Kilda branch of his long-lost relatives in Melbourne, the Solomons.

To that end I had already contacted them, supplied them with what I knew and a structured plan to ease his way in. They were appreciative of my efforts and said so in the many letters which travelled between the two states.

Samuel was third in line on the cousins list with the wealthy Solomons, who owned many music shops, had many New York contacts and would set Samuel up just after his eighteenth birthday. However, I did not want him to be the last to find out and it was drawing near to the time to feed him some information.

I called him into the office for a chat. 'Samuel…'

He sat forward listening, holding his cup of tea, but I saw his hands had a slight tremor.

'…we have spoken about your interest in many Jewish matters, haven't we?'

He pre-empted what I had to say. 'Allan, I know what you're going to tell me. My heart yells it out and I guessed a few years ago. Bloody hell, look at my nose. I was born a Jew! Wasn't I?'

'Yes, son.' I always called him son out of earshot of others.

He smiled at me with an expectant look. I produced from a dog-eared box the Star of David, still gleaming gold with the overhead light catching a reflection and shadows of the star cast on the opposite wall. Without any word, I handed it over to him.

A tear formed in the corner of his eyes as he clutched it and smelled it. 'I can smell, Allan. I can smell my mother. She's here now. Do you believe that?'

'Yes, I do, Samuel. I believe it.' I stood up and helped him place the icon around his neck. 'How does that feel now?'

He leaned back and fondled the old icon. 'I shall never take it off again.'

I produced more papers. His birth certificate nominated Norwood as his place of birth and gave his mother's name, but someone had scratched out the father.

'I wonder why. I wonder why,' he said.

Samuel, you're directly related to the Solomons in Melbourne. They have a job waiting for you as soon as you turn eighteen years of age. They also have a will concerning some inheritances which they will hand you. Would you like to live in Melbourne?'

He thought about it and said he would me miss me and his employers in Rundle Street but, yes, he would.

'The people in Rundle Street are also related to the Solomons and wish only the best for you. It will be a good move for you, Samuel.'

I thought it might have been too much yet he seemed to enjoy all the gifts coming his way, so I produced the Commonwealth savings bank book first started by his Uncle Harry with one thousand three hundred pounds in it, accessible after his birthday, which made him sit up and check the balance and compound interest. He was keen on compound interest, just like Einstein once remarked on.

'OK, son, come back tomorrow night and I'll fill you in with some of my journeys.'

He thanked me and skipped out of the office – and why wouldn't he, I thought.

The next night he arrived straight after work and on time. He was a punctual lad, which would augur well in his life. I poured him a cup of tea and we chatted.

'I was born in Marree in the far north and I grew up with camels and their drivers. I learned to ride them and liked the Afghan people. World War I broke out and I was recruited into the Camel Corps with the 1st Division and soon in the Middle East. I survived without a scratch and had no ties so I stayed in the Middle East and wandered around. I met a lot of Jewish people and came to love them, so that's why I have a connection. And why we're always on the same wavelength. I was also, as you know, a cello player but nowhere near as talented as you. That helped in those lands when I played for families at times. I thought about how outcast the Jews were and how mistreated they were but how tough they are as well. It's not that I ignored Jesus – he was, after all, a Jew – but I found a part in my life for both religions. I was out alone in the desert one night just walking and I felt a rush of warmth come over me. I looked up into the sky and I think I saw God and spoke to him. I never needed a priest after that because I could talk to him freely. I still do. I felt dizzy like something had left me, just like a snake sheds its skin. I was no longer a youth but an old wise man wrinkled with skin as dry as a hydrangea leaf. I wandered about walking with a soft tread and saw a seven-foot snake raring up at me. I stood still and breathed very shallowly as it passed over my old boot, slithering away in a zigzag pattern. I felt alone, almost homeless, with the prospect of a world changing too fast for my old bones A thought came into my mind of why humans have treated others with no significance since before the time of Jesus. A veil lifted and chased away my thoughts. My eyes lit on the beauty of the world, with the sky, the moon, the stars. And the desert became in that time a majestic place, which has not changed, and neither have my alternative views which have caused me some trouble over the years.'

Samuel sat staring in thought without any reply.

I produced my old Camel Corps hat bag with the rising sun and the camel emblazoned on it.

'I never knew about this, Allan.'

We both sat lost in our thoughts but the silence was soon broken when he did one thing which was just Samuel and something which was a virtual ritual that always broke the ice.

He pulled out his harmonica and played Vera Lynn's old World War II song, and I sang along. 'We'll meet again, don't know where, don't know when, but I know we'll meet again some sunny day.'

I hoped the lyrics would prove prophetic yet something told me it would not be in the flesh, rather that I might come back to him – with him on the piano and me on my cello.

6

Samuel

1956

The jigsaw of my life started to make sense after my new-found Auntie Gloria Solomon (née Harris) sent a pile of family photos in the mail, along with copious letters, a family tree and photos of all of the poor people (our close relatives) who died at the Nazis' bloody hands.

Some of the photos had unexpected puzzles: the wedding photo of my parents Aaron and Rachael certainly posed a puzzle. I instantly recognised Uncle Harry Samuels from his life and from my dreams. He was taller than his brother and leering behind Aaron with his black hair in a widow's peek, much darker than the groom and with a much bigger nose than Aaron's. There was a bugger-the-world expression on his face and his hands were on his hips, not held down at the side like the newly weds.

I was a born in 1938, so what happened that caused him to come into my small bedroom and look at me with blazing eyes? I quite clearly remember the word 'bastard' used in my face. And a Salvo kid told me what it meant. Was I born out of wedlock? It seemed to be the only excuse for using the word or was it because he felt tied down with a kid and was just swearing?

Auntie Gloria came to visit but seemed unwilling to explain it all and went on about the new friends I would meet in Melbourne. She lingered overly long on 'And of course there are the girls. Do you have a girlfriend, Samuel?'

Having grown into a smart arse, I was well aware of the implications and had been warned by Allan: 'Be careful of Gloria. She's a classic

Jewish mother and she'll have you lined up with a good Jewish girl as soon as possible.'

So I heeded his warning and was able to deflect her as diplomatically as I could. But it would take all of my intuition to keep her onside.

I promised myself a once-off simple journey on the Glenelg tram from Adelaide to the beach. It was a cheap indulgence and I had learned over my growing years to tackle simple tasks without delay. My bank book looked good because of my rigid savings plan and the tram trip would be pleasurable.

I never had a motorbike, never drank or smoked, and I didn't have a girlfriend yet I lied to Gloria that I did -- to keep her off my tail for a while. Maybe later in life I might meet a good Jewish girl and settle down – who knows.

The walk to town cleared my lungs of the silly cough which I had and I bought a ticket from the conductor on the tram and settled down for the trip on the hard timber seats, listening to the squeaks of the carriage and the squealing brakes at stops, and watching the panorama of suburbs as we passed by on the tracks.

We arrived at the terminus at Glenelg and the passengers got off. I stayed on, lost in my thoughts of Melbourne and the life which beckoned. No one else boarded for the return journey. There was only the conductor and me and he was smoking a cigar at the rear of the carriage. The smoke was aromatic and a tiny memory of the same aroma flooded into my head. At the same time, a great cold came over me with another irritating cough. My temperature rose to very hot and then subsided.

I heard a noise in the distance coming in loud. It was a harmonica playing 'Jerusalem'. It was a song which I had played many times with Allan in the Salvation Army band. I started to sing it but stopped when a woman who was now sitting opposite glared at me. Yet the instrument still played so I hummed it until the angry woman got off at the next stop.'

The wet wool smell came in strong this time. I did not turn round but I knew it was Uncle Harry sitting close by. I felt the gentle brush of a finger wiped across my face. A gravelly voice spoke into my right ear. 'Shalom, Samuel.' And the presence was gone.

I waved goodbye to it while it faded like bubbles popping from a child's bubble pipe. I had been pushed back into 1943 on a cold morning sitting on a cold seat. Some other passengers looked at me while I waved to what must to them have seemed an imaginary figure. But it was time. Time to entertain the tram audience.

I stood up with my harmonica poised at my lips and bowed. I started to play 'Now is the Hour'. Children stopped squirming. Babes in arms stopped drinking from their mothers' hidden breasts and the conductor used his ticket clipper to provide some percussion

I bowed at the end and took in the cheers and the applause. They were mine. I had captured my audience and I thought right then, 'Look out, Broadway. Here I come – the smell of the greasepaint, the roar of the crowd.' I danced a tap and the kids joined with me. So did the conductor.

In all of the performances which were to come I would always mark this one as my best. And it was free for the folk on that Glenelg tram. However, a man spontaneously passed around a hat which was filled with all sorts of change – even some US dimes and a couple of French francs, which topped up the bank book once again.

I had to tell Allan about the tram and the spirit as well. He believed in the spirit world and had seen evidence of it himself during his war service with the Camel Corps.

His remarks were comforting. 'He's your guide, whether it's out of guilt for your dumping I don't know, but you'll meet again many times in your life, Samuel, of that I'm sure.'

I thought on those words during the train trip to Melbourne later on.

7

Samuel

Melbourne

The Melbourne express rattled slowly past the last stop, Sunshine, before its destination. A green place, a cold place, yet it had trams clanking, winding, stopping, picking up passengers, and I sensed a buzz in the city which I never felt in Adelaide.

Sleep did not come on the train, though there were some quick dozes, before the guard called out, 'Last stop, Melbourne.'

I stretched and brushed my rough but clean clothes, which had been for me a second skin and a reminder of how far I had come since 1943. Many thoughts entered my overloaded mind during the last hours of the journey. Would I cope with a new family? Would I lose my last thirteen years of some solitude, making the best of everything without anyone having to pick me up? Yet there was Allan of course--- in a sense my spiritual father —and he above all would not be replaced, even by an inherited family. But I once more grounded myself by looking at the bank book and brushing my fingers over the entry showing compound interest.

There they were – the welcoming committee. A tall man with a black hat and a black beard held up a huge sign: 'Welcome home, Samuel.' A feeling of unease, a smothering cloud came into my presence which was bolstered the moment I saw the familiar figure of Gloria, racing intent on being at the head of the assembly to be, two steps in front of all with her right of passage.

I was still wobbly, having not stretched during the night, and I took a step back when the large woman with her blonde hair piled high, with dangly Star of David earrings, wearing a purple dress, decked with more gold than a princess, her hazel eyes flashing, ran up. Everyone stepped out of her path when she made the leap into my arms.

She was much heavier than I imagined and I couldn't hold her and there we were sprawled on the platform together with her lavender knickers emblazoned with purple butterflies and her very nice, shapely tanned legs exposed to all.

But she didn't care. She just cried then wiped her tears away with another cloth also with butterflies on it. Her rose perfume enveloped all the crowd who pulled us to our feet.

I instantly thought this was a Jewish mother to top all Jewish mothers.

The following half-hour trip to the Jewish quarter in St Kilda was a blur of parting handshakes, more questions than answers.

I was shown my downstairs room with a desk, a built-in robe and photos on the wall.

'Better here for you downstairs. You can come and go with your studies and the nights when you're late home from work, Samuel,' Gloria said in her high-pitched voice, still with her eyes flashing all over me.

She slid open the robes and there before me was an array of suits, sports coats, gaudy shirts and black Italian shoes. I stared at them and was reminded of Joseph's coat of many colours, and there I was in my worn clean old clothes.

She must have sensed something (Gloria always sensed something). 'When you've changed, bring down those old worn-clothes and I'll chuck them out.'

I did not answer. How could I discard my clothes? It was like discarding my life, chucked into long grass as carelessly as a ball is thrown away.

My stomach expanded each day. There would be a knock on the door, then a rush in with a tray piled high with coffee cakes and chocolates, and this went on for a week at least five times a day and all the time she sat watching my jaws chomping, nodding and anxiously asking, 'Good? Good? Good?'

I always said yes until I was able to corner Benjamin, her husband, a quiet man who knew what I meant.

But I understood another factor that was driving her. She had lost a son aged two years with German measles and I was the replacement. Other relatives visited and always said, 'Look at him – just like the boys.'

And I would look at Benjamin and smile.

There were quiet times (not many) during the night when I would muse about my changed circumstances and a little thought of ingratitude would be pushed away until it returned when I thought that Gloria was like a hurricane sucking all up in its path, especially me with my suitcase, my papers and my old clean clothes. Was she a giant vacuum cleaner, a hoover, I mused, and I would grin, then get up and look again at my bank book and settle down, dreaming up plans which were not on Gloria's radar beam.

I gazed at the wedding photo of my parents for hours. My mother at her best, and how I like to remember her with Aaron my father and Uncle Harry, taller than either of them, with his lanky looks and smirking smile and the prominent nose. I heard the sound of the old motorbike each time I picked up the photo. And there were many times.

I spoke to my relatives once about my life with the Salvos and Allan.

'He's a nice man,' Gloria said.

'My father, my guide really,' I added, which caused a few quick glances between them.

I told them about the tram trip and for once in the short time I had lived with Gloria and Benjamin she became silent and then serious.

'Harry comes to us in our dreams. He sends us messages.' She wiped her tears. 'I've overwhelmed you, Samuel, and for that I am sorry. It's just…it's just…' And the words drifted away.

I stood up and approached her and she looked at me with those hazel eyes which spoke of her love and devotion for her family I held her close and wiped her tears and glanced at quiet Benjamin, whose eyes were also glazed.

Our relationship became one of beloved nephew and aunt rather than mother and son. I tucked away my bank book because I was grounded. I did not need reminders of the good coming my way.

The will was in my hands. I read it at the house I inherited from Uncle Harry…just down the road. I looked in the garage and saw the motorcycle and sidecar, other old bikes and a 1930 Ford A still in remarkable condition.

'Harry was the favourite of Mary Solomon, who lived in New York and danced on Broadway. She left him this house and now it's yours.'

Judy and Sid Solomon, the newly weds, rented the place and looked after it, tending the old cottage gardens. Coffee and cake as usual came out.

Judy looked at me with the look of her Auntie Gloria. 'Are you going to sell this when you're twenty-one?'

I was thoughtful but shook my head, then added, 'Stay as long as you like. It looks as though you're looking after the place. The garden's marvellous '

They both smiled. The conversation stalled but I knew the way forward because I hadn't played for three weeks. Out came the harmonica and out came the music and on came the tap dance

'Bloody Harry's back again. Look at him.'

'Yes, Benjamin. But it's Mary and Rachael too, isn't it?'

One day maybe old Mary might come through to me. I hope so anyway. Yet there was other news when I opened a letter from Allan.

National Service had visited. I was to report for induction. Benjamin suggested that it could be deferred but I was determined I would let the process begin. It was three months at an army camp with basic training. I passed the medicals, breezed though the training, enjoyed it and saw mothers' boys crying, not coping. One hanged himself. If only they knew.

I walked through the lot and was urged to join the army band but declined. I made a few more friends and met some girls on weekend leave. My life was opened up. I think I changed from a growing boy into a man when I walked out with a few elephant stamps on my service record.

My job was a re-run of the Adelaide shop and I acquired more friends and skills.

The New York relatives from Eldridge Street in the lower east side had heard about me and started to ring. They enquired if I would like to live there and continue my studies.

I jumped at the chance. I was twenty years of age and the Big Apple was on my lips. It was my next punt in the world of gambles which, in Aussie slang, would pay off, I reckon. I had won the daily double.

A bar mitzvah, a real fair dinkum Jewish affair, was on the cards in spite of the fact that I had long ago passed thirteen, which was the traditional age. Yet I had some reservations and had to keep silent about the duality of my beliefs.

8

Samuel

Dancing With Harry

New York, the Sixties

Harry was with me all the way, not on the plane but outside, tap dancing on clouds and at times watching them fade, somersaulting, joyous and I thought, 'It must be as good as it is spoken about in that other world,' but I never asked him in my many dreams the questions which would be expected of us occupiers of the planet…like do you eat, even do you shit, make love and have you seen God or met your parents?'

As a result of those dreams and insightful talks with Harry (and some tap as well), he decided we ought to make a pact for this last journey to New York for me (and him). So we did and it was to last for a decade and then he would go in a blink one night to some other plane.

It was 3 January 1960 and I felt comforted with his presence and his knowledge of the world I had chosen to enter with the assistance of the Jewish connection. I hummed many tunes all the way on the long flight and saw he was still there clinging to a porthole like a hitchhiker. Why he hung on outside is beyond my knowledge but I do know it kept me entertained all the way and Harry, I am told, was a born entertainer.

He was there in Eldridge Street in the lower east side Jewish quarter sitting on the steps at the entrance to my flat. I opened the door with my key given by the generous New York Solomons once again and said to him as I flopped, 'OK, Uncle, we're here. Let's get started,' which meant rearranging furniture, hanging photos, walking past the piano and plonking a few chords which turned into a song, and his happy feet started again. It was fun for me. I was not scared now about the spirit who fully materialised when thunder and lighting struck and I never asked why that was so.

Harry was there in most of my dreams and his nose was always in the bevelled edge of the bathroom mirror, yet when the nose apparition was covered with steam his eyes did a dance up and down, side to side, just like an eye test when the optician instructs those movements.

But it was not all comedy and dance routines. Because when I sat composing, playing a chord or two, he would put up his harmonica and say (while alongside of me on the stool), 'Try it like this,' and I would watch as the keys were depressed – by a phantom hand. He would whisper good advice about security such as Walk in the middle of the road. Better still, hop with me. Lock your front door, double bolt it. This is a tough place.' I took his advice always and it worked

His happy feet were with me during the bar mitzvah, which came on with a rush. No mention was made before or after of my absence on my thirteenth birthday and I guess they all knew why. Everyone did who knew me, because it was the worst-kept secret in New York. Not that I cared anyway.

I swore oaths on the Torah and promised not to break them and to keep sacred texts in certain places. It concluded with the Tefillin ceremoniously wound around my hands and that was it.

The graduation ceremony of my scholarship was over. I was in the music writers' world and a circle of people of the same ilk came into my life. And Harry was there all the time with his advice. In between the copious writing, I studied photo journalism. Harry thought I had talent and it was a fall-back position in times of writer's block. 'Freeing the mind' are the words he used. That venture brought about many photo gigs through parts of the USA for a large and glossy Jewish magazine.

We tapped down south and danced back quicker than we came because the good old boys didn't like Jews or interlopers from the north. It was so racist and very tangible – so much so that it could be cut with a knife. I have not returned to the land of magnolias and the heavy, humid climates

My first real sexual encounter came and continued for a few months till she either found better prospects or pastures or I was doing something wrong. Even though I asked Harry to stay clear during this phase, he would occasionally cackle when Jillian was in the bed with me and off she would run to the bathroom only to be confronted with Harry's nose in the bevelled edge. It didn't take too long to unwind after that.

He watched once I found a taste for the 'juice', as the New Yorkers say. I found some escape and warmth in the booze but I knew Harry did not approve. He would not have approved of my cocaine habit in the seventies – decidedly not. But he was not around then to judge.

New York city is a place where you can't expect a handout. However, the opportunity to succeed, no matter where you are or where you come from, is there begging you to go for it. I felt the pride and the elegance of the city and quickly saw how its citizens loved the place. It's my city too, my Broadway, and Harry shared those ten years with me in dancing and dreams. I wonder whether the dream is reality or is it vice versa. I don't linger on those thoughts. There are more pressing matters. I just plough forward.

We danced in sad times as well, especially when JFK was shot, and when Martin Luther King was killed, yet our feet tapped a dignified percussion sounding like muffled drums combined with the clip-clop of horses' hooves.

Harry was there when the Beatles and other groups took over and dampened old Broadway. But Broadway is constant…it has never left. Broadway is New York and New York is Broadway: it can't be kept down for long.

We heard the soul music, Motown, and knew disco was coming –

all of those styles had an impact on my work. As did Liza Minelli Peter Allen, the Rat Pack, and Bob Fosse, the great choreographer, but I don't want to sound like a name dropper.

The decade was closing yet Harry still danced in the middle of the street until I saw a bleeding New York city cop lying prone on the side walk. His gun lay beside him, I checked his pulse, which was beating. His eyes flicked open. I shoved my hand on the slashed shoulder to stop the blood.

A shadow came from behind and I turned around. A crazy man with eyes wide open held a machete over his head and was very close.

I picked up the policeman's .38 Smith and Wesson and fired two shots right into the groin of the crazy man. He screamed and fell and within seconds I heard the sounds of the sirens.

Patrolman Ed Ryan recovered. I had visited him and the press were everywhere. Despite my struggle with having to shoot the man, the whole episode gave to me huge publicity. Agents, record companies wanted to know about the Aussie bloke who wrote songs, tutored students and was also a photo journalist.

The New York City Police gave me a bravery citation and I was made an honorary cop. I went to the precinct and was roundly applauded.

A senior patrolman spoke. 'Samuel Samuels saved the life of one of our guys. He could have walked away but he didn't. Instead he fired two shots into the perp's balls and blew them off. What do you think of that, eh?'

Everyone laughed and Harry did as well. We all got thoroughly sloshed on Murphy's beer delivered in big containers and supplied by grateful citizens.

The headlines revealed that Ed had accidentally stumbled on a drug drop and the other person involved took off with the bag of money, which caused the mad man to go berserk.

New Year's Eve came and I was drunk. I woke up with a massive hangover and headed to the bathroom. I gazed in the mirror but there was no sign of Harry and then I remembered. It was 1 January 1970. Harry had danced out of my life in New York city. He must be with other spirits, I thought. Yet I knew I would need him again one day, especially now that, with the possibility of war in the Middle East, I had signed on to cover stories in Israel.

I made some trips back and forth with photos, so not much was written in those early years of the 1970s.

9

Samuel

Yom Kippur, 1973

When 1973 loomed, I was wearing green fatigues. I was attached to a forward platoon of Israel national service men approaching the Golan Heights.

We had been there for a while, living in and around the British-made Centurion tank with the fog of war draped over us like a giant balloon. The balloon would not have shrunk from us even if we pushed it away: it would just spring into another direction, so we lived with it until the shells came.

Yom Kippur happens to be the holiest day of the Jewish calendar. The Muslims share the same day with their Ramadan and the combined forces of Syria and Egypt must have concluded what an opportunity to get rid of the accursed Jews once and for all on that day when they attacked on 6 October.

How did we survive it? God knows and so does General Moshe Dayan with the romantic black patch over one eye: a man of economical speed but each word he spoke to the microphones thrust in his face was repeated throughout the land. His most memorable answer to how he achieved his success in battle was 'It helps to have the Arabs on the other side.'

I never heard those lines when he first spoke them because I was in a hospital in Tel Aviv, badly wounded, despite my non-combatant status.

Syria had 1,400 tanks; we had 180. Egypt's 600 000 troops and 555 planes were massed along the Suez. (They always went for overkill, like Rameses, and look where it got him.)

My images and articles rushed to New York told how modern this war was. I knew the country would be cheering and dancing along with each news report from the Middle East.

Yet there were lulls at times between the action when cleaning gear and playing cards filled the spaces. I helped fill those spaces when I was urged to play a few tunes and dance with the men of my platoon. Out came the harmonica, which had to wiped to dislodge the dust.

However, the music stopped suddenly when fear crept in as a collective silence of impending doom came upon us. The metallic sound of clunk clunk and then the boys hitting the ground yelling, 'Mortars, mortars'… and they rained on us. It was over in minutes. I thought I had peed myself but when I looked I saw blood pouring into my boot. I folded up and passed out, luckily before the pain came.

A truck ground to a halt, doors slammed and people in white coats gathered around while I was pushed into the bright lights of the Tel Aviv hospital.

In those seconds, the pain flashed into my back and legs and I clamped my jaw shut to not cry or yell. Other soldiers were yelling all around the emergency ward, making enough noise not to need my contribution too.

I hardly felt the prick of the pain-killing injection and I was by then in a fuzzy world of no recognition.

Days passed until I really knew where I was.

'We might have found the trouble, Samuel.' A woman named Joanne had just finished massage. Joanne was in her army greens with a small submachine gun slung over her shoulder. Medics fought as well in Israel in this war.

A doctor came in at the same time she left.

I knew what she meant. I was nosey and read the medical chart which said, 'Source isolated and controlled with antibiotics.' I had one kidney left and broken ribs. I had been close to death for weeks.

Doctor Simon looked excited and I had to look surprised when he told me I was in recovery. But there were more tests and intrusions with painful injections to follow. So on the down side I was not out of the woods.

I had to have a colonostomy to check out my bowel. They wheeled me into surgery and put a mask over my face. I knew from my readings that a small camera would be soon circling from my anus to the bowel.

The staff giggled when one said, 'He ought to be used to cameras.'

I opened my eyes. 'Not up my arse, you morons.' I was soon in la la land. But I bet their attempt at humour at my expense was curtailed.

They didn't find anything up there, no swallowed pennies, no chewed scripts or an ID swallowed in case we were captured, or that my hat was on straight as was the standard joke in the ward.

Apart from a serious morphine addiction, I was out with a program of therapy to follow for months, which went on even when I landed back in Melbourne for a while. I expected that I would receive the full treatment from Gloria and Benjamin and I did.

Their loving care pulled me through and along with their care came the daily messages from the New York Solomons eagerly awaiting my return.

My job was waiting for me so, like the wandering Jew, my faltering steps, stiff-legged but straight once again, walked the streets of the lower east but not in the middle of the road this time.

However, baggage in the form of addiction travelled with me. I smoked a joint each night as well and wondered what Patrolman Ed Ryan would think about me now. Would I still be the honorary cop? I guessed Harry would not approve but he wasn't there to guide me, or so I thought.

Sarah came into my life at the clinic which I attended. She was a Jewish woman, never married and a writer of children's books. We shared much – as well as an addiction. She had been a nurse in the US Army in Saigon during the Vietnam War and her nightly horrors were real and draining.

It was unsung, not spoken about. We were on the same plane and got together in a close relationship. It helped us both because we wanted to control our addictions. Yet there were times when it was too much, when the writer's block came in,when we fell into bed at three a.m. after knocking off a bottle of Jack Daniels, smoking a joint, making love and falling into a snoring dreamless sleep. Then woken by the punching on walls from next door. 'Stop your goddam snoring.' We would just turn over on our sides and snore again but with less noise.

Oh, and we got married, without any formalities, with just a few guests. No honeymoon, we were too busy, and it would have meant if we had gone away there would be more nights of waking up the next people in a motel.

A noisy night came and went and Sarah had gone to her office. I was shaving and cleaning out the whiskers from the bowl when I saw the bevelled edge of the mirror with eyes looking straight at me. Harry was back in my life once again.

10

Bicheno, Tasmania, 1975

Joe came through his war of the forties and the occupation of Japan, Korea and Vietnam, where it all ended, with an honourable discharge, a good pension and a Japanese war bride named May. There were no signs of distress on the face of the former warrant officer and many put it down to his fishing boat and the solitude he felt as a result, and his love of family – he had one son named Jake, who was a second engineer with the P&O cruise line.

Yet the secrets which Harry Samuels and he jointly shared were of concern in the vivid dreams of late. Dreams which had him holding Harry in death, and then there was the bottle with the secrets.

May kept him grounded with her care and he loved her from the time they first met in Kure. Her mother reluctantly gave permission for her only daughter to marry, since her father had been killed in Borneo. Joe sometimes wondered if he was at the beach on that dreadful day in 1945 at Balikpapan. She still wore the silk kimono which had been given to her as a present but only at home because for a time in 1950 she encountered some racism and Joe was fighting in Korea then. She had Jake to care for and spent most days at home in their beachside house at Bicheno which Joe and his friends built all those years ago. However, the racism soon faded when she sold her embroidery at the many Market stalls nearby.

On his way out for his usual walk, Joe yelled, 'Walking, May.'

'OK, Joe.'

'Goodbye, Jake.' He winked at the photo of his son on the hall table in his ensign uniform and strolled out the door.

Joe sat at the rocks near the blowholes with Ted, his black kelpie, at his side. It was a brisk afternoon and the sun would soon be setting. He loved to watch the sunset.

I'm blessed in my life, he thought. He turned back to his old religion of the Methodists and thanked God in his thoughts. He asked God to protect Jake overseas and at sea and hummed 'Amazing Grace' softly.

Although he had dreamed a lot more in retirement, he had just flickering visions of Harry and his mouth organ. Harry played 'Amazing Grace' many times, yet Joe had not heard it played for sometime until that morning when the strains of the mouth organ came through as he sat gazing at the sun in the west. In that moment after an absence of thirty years he felt a presence nearby.

'Harry, Harry, is it you? Are you there?'

Ted whimpered. He was restless. He sat up and barked a small bark. Just one small bark. He trotted off to a rock some yards away and looked back at Joe. The dog started to scratch at the wet sand, stopping, looking at Joe, begging him to come and look.

And Joe did. Joe dug further down and saw the gleam of a green glass bottle. He picked it up, washed it in the sea and saw clearly on the bottom of the glass 'Pickaxe brand' and he knew then this was the bottle thrown into the sea thirty years ago.

He did not amble back this time. He ran, tripping falling yet still holding tightly onto the precious cargo. He ran into the front door with Ted at his heels, puffing at the breakfast bar.

'Joe, Joe, what's the matter?' May was used to his casual strolls and his beachcombing but this was a preserved old bottle with something inside it.

Joe sat for a while until he found an opener and carefully prised the bottle open. There before his eyes were all the papers which Harry had locked away the night before the beach assault.

The smell of war, of gun oil, of canvas, engulfed him, causing his heart to race at a gallop. He took charge with a few deep breaths and read the thirty-year-old material. Light beamed through their kitchen window though the afternoon was cloudy. May had been told about the bottle and she knew about ghosts in her family. She thought that the spirit of Samuel had led Joe to the bottle. She knew he was going to cry and she held his shoulders while he sobbed. He had never cried apart from when they married and when Jake was born, but this time he could not stop the flood.

May passed him a glass of water which he downed in one gasping gulp.

It was then that he spoke. 'I don't know if it was God but this is amazing. None one will ever rail against God to me in the future,' and then he added, 'Yes, old mate, I will find him for you.'

Ted came up to Joe and stood on his hind legs as if he knew about the contents; he was the finder of the bottle after all.

Joe bent down and picked Ted up in his arms, which was not something he ever did. 'Big bone for you tonight, mate.'

And Ted ran around in circles knowing something good was going to happen. He sat at his bowl, his tail wagging expectantly. He took the bone outside and chased away the next-door neighbour's cat.

Joe began at the beginning. He was sent material from Allan Parsons of the Salvation Army with the addresses of the child Samuel Samuels. The gaps were filled by the Solomons of St Kilda.

A meeting was to happen in Melbourne but before the revealing moments that would surely eventuate he took a trip to Canberra to remember and speak to Harry at the memorial to the fallen soldiers of Balikpapan.

11

Samuel

Melbourne, November 1975

Sarah chatted for hours on the phone to Gloria, who thanked her for caring for her wounded nephew, and as a result I rang St Kilda and asked if we could visit.

The request was warmly received, though I detected a hint of disappointment in her voice for not having been invited to a great Jewish wedding. However, I was able to reassure her she was not forgotten and explained how we had wanted a very small short informal occasion. Our need for privacy was paramount.

Gloria was never to be told the real reason, which was our narcotics habit. We had to kick it without prying eyes or ears. A big reception might have uncovered the addiction which was our shame.

We set off for Australia leaving a freezing winter behind. Sarah was in and out of the toilet just before we came into Melbourne. There she was, in a tizz, rushing in and out of the toilet splashing perfume in order to make a grand entrance on arrival.

'Good,' I said when she made her last dash. 'Settle down, for God's sake. You smell like a New York flower stall.'

But she wasn't listening because she had out her compact mirror applying blusher and her lippie (she always laughed at our Aussie way of shortening words).

Then she looked at me. 'Is there any lipstick on my teeth?'

But I just laughed. Her temperature had been raging since we left the Big Apple and my concern was for her well-being, not for appearances.

We landed and went to the turntable for our luggage and there was Mike Solomon, another cousin, walking over with a look of the Solomons stamped all over his face. We hugged, kissed and went to his car. Small conversations of really nothing punctuated the air on the drive to St Kilda.

I gained the impression he was holding back something but never pushed the envelope. This was not just a social visit: something else was in the air. And there it goes – my bloody intuition, which bugs me at times, which has been wrong more times than I care to remember of late. I put that down to the yippie beans I'm taking, a habit which has got to stop.

They rushed to greet us like a pack of meerkats with shiny eyes and heads bobbing up – like they all expected some curious news, I thought at the time. This had better be good

Benjamin opened up first. After the traditional hugs and kisses and the 'How have you been?' 'How was the flight?' and 'Goodness, Sarah, you're hot. Have these,' he produced some aspirins with a glass of water.

Sarah gulped them down.

Benjamin's brief but careful explanation of how the bottle came into the Solomons' hands was concluded when he handed me all the papers which had been inside the old bottle.. They had had to open it up. It was no point asking us to come over if it was just gibberish or destroyed. But I did not take umbrage at others reading the stuff before me.

I read the small card first with 'SHALOM, SAMUEL' written neatly with scrolls and whorls, and I smelt it. I knew it had been written by Harry. I smelt the sea yet a musty smell was there too, which I suppose should be expected seeing it was thirty years old.

Gloria never interrupted except to say, 'This is for your eyes now, though we had to read it. Outside of Benjamin and me, you are the next one. It is, after all, addressed to you.'

I read on and then had to put it down because a buzzing came into my right ear just after I read the lines of how Harry was sad that he dumped me in 1943. The buzzing stopped and I heard a female voice speaking in the still quiet room where one could hear a pin drop. It was sharp, clear and to the point.

'Please don't judge me, Samuel.'

I must have surprised everyone in the room when I replied to the voice of my mother, which I had never forgotten. It used to be lilting and funny until she became sick and drunk. Even a three-year-old knows and remembers.

'OK, Mum. Just let me read this.' The buzzing stopped.

I read to the critical words: 'I am your father…not your uncle.'

I dropped the paper. This was not what I expected.

Gloria was watching the expressions change on my face. I picked up the papers once again, anxious to read what else he had to say.

'I fell in love with your mother – we made love only once while Aaron was away with his work. She was lonely. She became pregnant. My sin has haunted me up till now.' I had no tears, just thoughts which raced. I understood why Aaron kept calling me 'bastard'. The pieces of the puzzle fitted. I stood up.

Sarah had a firm grip on my hand. 'Do you mind if we go to our room?'

And they made way while we went upstairs.

Sarah closed the windows and the curtains. We had need of some weed, which we smoked until the early hours.

In unison we read each other's thoughts and felt the hand of God was in the miracle of the bottle reaching the finder Joe Bedford. We also concluded that we would, as soon as possible, return to our church, and to that end we went down on our knees and prayed for the first time in many months. There were no more secrets to be revealed and I was glad of it. Although we were childless, we would be OK. We needed to go cold turkey, a thought which was prominent in our minds on that night.

'What are you doing today, my children?' Gloria considered us to be her kids in a way, which I understood.

I shrugged and looked at Sarah.

Gloria took the reins once again. 'Joe Bedford is on the way over from Tasmania. Come with us to the ferry.'

I had no hesitation. This was the man who last saw my father alive all those years ago.

We were late or the ferry was early and there they were. Joe with his Japanese-born wife May with a placard around her neck. My memories of placards made me wince.

They walked towards us and, after shaking hands with all of us, Joe looked me over, his bright brown eyes appraising me as he looked up from his stocky five feet eight into my lanky six feet three.

'Yep, you're Harry's lad, that's for sure.' He put his hand in his pocket and pulled out a well preserved harmonica with Harry's initials inscribed which he handed to me along with Harry's service record, a photo of the inscription on the stone of those men who died at the beach landing and Harry's bayonet, which he had swiped at the beach later on. I gazed at the thirty-odd-year-old artefacts.

It was appropriate to play something on the mouth organ. A couple of slides to oil it up and then I played 'Waltzing Matilda'. People gathered around. Many sang it and those who didn't clapped at the end of my impromptu performance

Joe turned around and saw a man wearing World War II medals. 'This lad's father, my mate, died in Borneo.'

The man nodded walked over and shook my hand. 'I guess you wouldn't remember him, though, would you?'

I had to be careful about my answer. 'I knew him well, actually, and I've seen his spirit many times.'

The man smiled and handed me a card. 'Visit me if you wish or phone me. I'm a spiritualist. I became one after the war. I wanted answers and I sure as hell got them.'

I was not sure I wanted answers but Sarah was different, because her trips to mediums years ago had brought her accurate information. She rang the man later, made an appointment with him and came away with startling news which in my opinion was just poppycock. He saw her holding a baby boy who would be named Isaac and we would live in Israel. I just dismissed it.

Joe filled in the spaces about Harry for me in the next few days and rustled up out of his backpack a photo of the both of them standing together, which I treasured.

'I guess you know the secret now. Have you forgiven him?'

I smirked just like Harry did.

He said, 'Good. Well done, lad. He was a bit of a larrikin, your dad, but, shit, he could dance and play anything. He kept as alive with his stories. A laugh a minute was our Harry.'

Joe's eyes started to cloud over. It seemed that the more he flashed back to Harry the more it opened his emotions and with that came the tears. They tumbled down many more times over the next few days.

I said goodbye to him later and promised to stay in touch though it was never to happen.

Harry was returning to me again in dreams and was now calling me 'Son.' I didn't mind. I needed his advice anyway.

I had a view that we should sell the house and to that end we worked together everyday for weeks, painting, scrubbing, washing. The hard work made us both fit and helped us reduce our consumption of morphine. We walked a lot during that time, caught trams and sat in wonderful street cafés, just happy to watch the passing parade of people.

We pondered whether we should give living in Israel a go. It was, after all, our spiritual home. We needed advice from a rabbi before we made a decision.

I walked along the streets of Carlton searching for a hardware shop with someone who could show me what I wanted. I passed by a Salvation Army store and just out of curiosity peeped inside because it had been years since I'd been able to go in one. I thought about Allen while I was stuck in the doorway and then saw a figure in a Salvo uniform running towards me. It was Tom Watson, my young mate from those days in the home. Although we had sent cards to each other from year to year, I had not seen him or heard of him for a while.

He rushed up and almost fell in my arms. I stared at him for a short time and saw the purple burn mark on the side of his face.

'I'm good, Sam. I'm good. The purple is from Vietnam. Got caught in a crossfire.'

I knew he had served there but did not know much about it. He had not spoken about it in his cards.

'How are you, mate? Never thought I'd see you in that uniform.'

'Uniform fixation, Sam. Couldn't help myself. It's a long story. Glad I caught you. Did you know Allan died a few weeks ago?'

I stood there. I must have looked shocked and put my head down to hold back any tears. 'He was my best mate. Almost my father, Tom.'

His eyes registered what I had said. 'We didn't know where you were but his last words were for you, mate.'

I sobbed a cracked sob right then. Tom held me to his chest.

'Cancer?'

He waved his hands in the sky. 'Yep. God took him. The grand old man. You know he bashed old Melon Head after he found out what the rat did to me.'

'That would be Allan. I heard Melon Head went to gaol. Had a stroke.'

'Yep. Then died. Sorry to say it, God.' Tom looked upwards. 'Good riddance to bad rubbish. I mixed with a bad crew after he raped me. I went off the rails and did a stretch in the Magill Boys' Home and then I joined the army.'

'We've all suffered in our own ways, mate. But glad to see you came out the other end.'

'He did terrible things to me, Sam, selfish things with those fat fingers which filled me with hate. Maybe I've forgiven him. That's what we Salvos are supposed to do, but I still don't know…he had to pay somehow.'

'No whistle-blowers then, Tom. We just coped.'

Tom changed the subject. 'He wanted his ashes spread in Jerusalem.' Tom looked at with a quizzical look.

I had no hesitation. 'Get them to me. We're planning a trip back there. It might be permanent.'

Tom rushed away and came back with an urn.' This is it. Are you sure?'

'Give them to me. I'll do it. I'd be honoured. If it hadn't been for Allan, I don't know where I'd be in life.'

There was one final hug and I walked away forgetting about the hardware store, looking back once at Tom as he ambled back into the shop. Poor bugger, I thought…still suffering.

'Sarah, I'm home. Did you find a rabbi?

'Yep. Young, married, had two kids, open-minded and fervent. Got an appointment on Wednesday. OK?'

'Good, mate, good. Yep.' I had a few questions to ask this young married priest with two kids, an open-minded fellow with a fervent air. Sarah was always descriptive about people. I guess it came with her writing ability.

12

Samuel

Meeting the Rabbi

He welcomed us in and invited us to sit down on comfortable chairs and I saw all the pictures of priests and kings. Surprisingly, there was a picture of Jesus, which I stared at for a while.

He read my thoughts. 'Jesus was a Jew as well but people use him to promote their own agenda.'

I sat up. This was a man I could talk to.

Sarah's lips parted as they do when she is about to ask a question or speak. She did the talking while Rabbi Peter Golda listened intently with his fervent, piercing violet eyes. She stopped for a breath.

'It's a lovely story. It is a miracle or a masterful bit of serendipity from God.'

She was silent and Peter took up the cudgels once again.

'You must have loved Allan Parsons, Samuel.'

I did not have to reply. My looks replied for me.

'Tell me about what the medium said.'

'That Sarah would have a child, a boy, but it's impossible actually.'

'Nothing is impossible under God's laws.' He stood and brought back a copy of Genesis chapter 17 paragraph 17. 'Have a read of it now, out loud, please.'

Which we did. I had some doubts about it, though, after I read it.

'Abraham had a talk with God. God told him that Sarah (though old) would conceive and child would be named Isaac. It was a miracle and it happened. Will you trust in God from this moment on?'

We looked at each other and said in unison, 'Yes, Rabbi, we will.'

We had to pray for the next three weeks together at the same time. Which we did. We obeyed.

Two months later

Sarah just phoned from the surgery. Her voice was jubilant. When she spoke, her voice was full of her quiet resolve.

'We are going to have a baby in seven months. We'll name him Isaac, Sam.'

And it came to pass in 1979. Before that event, I tipped the rest of the weed down the toilet.

Nine months later

Here we are gazing down at the gift of God. Isaac is our golden-haired boy. I remember the words of Genesis. We thank God a lot more nowadays.

We hope his life will be long and fulfilling. However, we're anxious parents and sleep does not come easily because we wake up at his tiniest sound. I could not look at the circumcision and had to run outside.

Gloria's phone bill will soon get a lot higher because we plan to take Isaac to live in Israel. As it should be.

13

Tel Aviv

Spring 2000

We danced the new millennium in and I thought that Harry might appear because it was the year of his only grandson's twenty-first birthday. Maybe he sensed something; some impending doom which kept him away from being interrogated by his son. Or maybe he was just too upset to hang around.

2000 was my worst year as it turned out: nothing surpasses it, not even the events leading up to 1943. The winter had gone, its sharp winds causing citizens to turn up their collars and dive deep in their pockets. But I never felt the change of seasons, let alone cared about the cold, because I wanted to die and be with Isaac from the moment the doctor stood in his surgery gear and shook his head.

I turned my back and walked away, leaving Sarah to face the music of the swishing machines to which he was hooked as it faded down to a flat-line sound.

Bloody fucking meningitis. Just a bloody mosquito. No hero's death for my son, which his lifelong warrior ambition might have granted him. No flags, no muffled drums, no shots being fired.

God didn't stick around either. He just shot through like me, not at my left side where he usually gave out his thoughtful advice, maybe stroking his chin. Nothing majestic was delivered at all. So I gave him the flick.

I blamed everyone and everything, even Sarah for turning off the switch. Why couldn't she wait? He was born a miracle. Why couldn't God help him and make another one? I also blamed Israel for some wild reason. It locked in my brain and it would not go away.

In that last round of blames, Sarah and I fell out of kilter. I sank, she got on with it. I marooned myself in the study for weeks and she slipped cups and small dishes through the dog flap. My weight plunged from ninety-five kilos to seventy-five and I looked like a refugee from hell.

My last madness, before men came in bleached white suits to take me away, was when I turned Isaac's photos inwards to stare at the wall instead of me.

Yet in those bad days I became sneaky (after they let me out, bursting with all sorts of coloured pills sloshing around in my empty belly). I saw Sarah had marked on the calendar five days away with her writers' group.

I struck. The agent in the Big Apple rang me back after I booked a one-way flight to the city. He also sent me a picture by fax of the flat which he had rented. Simple one-bedroom in a high-rise in Manhattan. A piano was included.

I never left a card for Sarah. Just a curt note. 'Gone to New York.' No love, no nothing, in spite of her cooking for a week and putting stuff in the freezer for me. I was a shithead then and cared for no one.

The flight was a re-run of January 1960, I realised when I woke up with a start. There he was clinging to the porthole, not smiling this time, not dancing on clouds this time, just wearing a mournfll look which showed the dried tears sitting with the snot on the end of his big hooter.

I knew I was in trouble with Harry this time.

The orchestra

Days slipped away and the months dissolved like bubbles from a child's pipe and in my solitude I reviewed my life, including my shabby treatment of Sarah. I wrote her a letter of apology and asked if she would like to re-commence some sort of dialogue.

She rang back one night and we talked, or rather I just listened to her anger and then her tears. A reconciliation finally seemed possible to mend our fractured relationship. I booked a plane trip for her, not immediately but when she felt up to it. I wasn't pushing my barrow any more. Done enough of that, I thought.

Harry bobbed back this time. No mirrors, just a full materialisation in the room, standing cross-legged, resting his arm on the mantelpiece, grinning his happy grin and slightly starting to tap his feet. Some nights we would say nothing but just watch DVDs. My favourite, which I played over and over, was *All That Jazz*, the veiled story of Bob Fosse's life (I knew the testy but brilliant perfectionist).

I was more than obsessed with how the script writer snuck in the near death stages written about by Elizabeth Kubler-Ross after her studies with dying people. It occurred to me that I might have died or even be dead. Whatever, I had passed the stage of denial and making bargains with God. I was finding my own acceptance of death or near death.

Harry had grown sick of endlessly watching the same DVD and was tinkling with the keys. In that instant I saw what I would describe as an orchestra pit full of dead musicians,waiting for a conductor and they did not have long to wait.

Allan Parsons entered to the sound of applause and winked at me. He shook hands with Harry and waved his baton and the music played was straight from the angels. I was lost in a range of music from Beethoven to the Beatles and time flew by.

Just when the instruments were being picked up I saw in the back row, with a cello, Isaac. I jumped up and stumbled towards him but he held out his hand like a traffic cop. I was stopped by that invisible power and watched him fade away till the room was silent.

But then the sound of the orchestra started again and I watched as a chorus line of long-legged Broadway girls danced in with high kicks. They were being led arm in arm by Bob Fosse and Peter Allen singing 'Every thing old is new again'. They danced away, waving to me with their top hats.

Was I dead? No, I wasn't. Was it a dream? Maybe, but if it was, it was a beautiful dream. I whispered a thank you to Harry afterwards and asked him if he would pass on my love to Allan. I reckon he would have.

Harry and Allan arranged it, of that I'm sure, and it set my feet once again on the road to recovery, which was rapid when Sarah arrived in August 2001.

I had much to tell her. She was intent on resuming her writing and had put aside children's books because she now wanted to make it in the world of adult books and New York was just the place for that. So, without her knowledge, I contacted my agent and sent him some of her work. I hoped she wouldn't be angry about my intervention.

14

The Twin Towers, Manhattan

11 September 2001

The population of the bustling city went about their business with not the slightest hint of the tragedy which would soon envelop them and cast a pall of misery lasting for eternity. But then the mayor, emergency services, the governor and higher had no hint either.

Samuel Jacobs Samuels, born of Jewish heritage, an orphan who had triumphed over huge adversity with the help of some caring people and the spirit world, and his recently reconciled wife Sarah, also of the same race, were blissfully living their quiet lives in the tough world of writing, for which they both shared a love.

Samuel, newly devoted to his pragmatic wife, need not have been anxious to please her. They shared the old stuff nowadays before the great blip in their lives, when they lived in Israel. They took each minute, each hour, day by day flowing along with life. With their renewed love and appreciation of the joys of life which Samuel had lost for a time, money and driven ambitions were not within their framework.

Although Samuel had turned his back on God (which Sarah never did), his faith was renewed by the mainly unseen yet watchful Harry Samuels. Harry did not appear in the flesh sitting and watching DVDs when his son was in a huge mess. There was no need now that Sarah was here and standing by Samuel.

'Going to buy our lunch, Sam. Bagels. Do you like them with salami still?' she asked. 'Sick of writing for a while. Got the cramp in my fingers.'

'OK, love,' he called back and played a note on the piano. A familiar voice, 'No, son. Try this.' And he watched as a white key was depressed by an unseen hand and smirked the same smirk as his father did.

He stood up and shoved the writing under the stool, thinking Sarah would not like that bit of untidiness, and promised to pick it up before she returned. He walked towards the vast window staring down on the citizens from the Twin Towers.

A huge explosion came into his senses with flame, wind and smoke which caused him to jump back. The blast followed, blowing away the glass, and with it came a huge wind of flying debris which struck his whole body.

Blackness, dust and a lack of oxygen caused by the sucking flames took his breath as he was flung under the piano stool and mixed up with the shredded final material written over a few nights.

Death, which he had escaped over many years,took his life on that day of chaos.

Sarah was reduced to ashes by the flames which incinerated people jammed together in lifts. They never found her body

Firemen searched as many floors as they could access. They were like white ghosts moving about in the blackness with torches growing dimmer by the hour in the eerie Dante's *Inferno* atmosphere.

'John, quick. Here,' a voice called and John picked his way over carefully, fearful of falling steel struts capable of trapping and killing a human. They looked down at the piano stool and saw the shattered body of man, pale and covered in the dust and with no visible sign of life.

A stretcher was quickly found and just when Samuel was being loaded, an object fell out of his hand. They picked it up and wiped it clean. It was an old Australian Army hat badge with a camel in the centre of the rising sun. Inscribed at the bottom were the words 'CAMEL CORPS'.

'Never seen one of these, John. Looks like World War I.'

But John was busy searching for identification. He found an Israeli passport, a medal for valour from the New York City Police and an evocative note old and yellowed with the words 'SHALOM, SAMUEL' written with elegant loops and whirls.

John was also a New York city born and bred Jewish man. He stood and looked down and in that moment both the men thought they heard the strains of the Israeli national anthem being played by a mouth organ. John stood stiffly to attention and saluted and his friend saw the tears which streaked down the white dust of his face.

They took Samuel's body away very carefully and told the NYPD captain what they found.

Captain Ed Ryan looked at the body of his rescuer and remembered how his life had been saved by the writer of music. He took off his cap and kneeled down, crossing himself ,and then cried a little till there were no more tears left.

He wanted to say the words 'Shalom, Samuel' but his throat was choked with dust.

John knew, though, and spoke the words for the captain.

Epilogue

A Respite Nursing Home

Melbourne, 2004

Gloria Solomon, a widow now after some years, sat on her bed, brushing the photos scattered on the single-room bed. There was a bathroom within easy reach: she had more need of it since the bladder cancer had returned. Among the photos of many weddings was a male toddler and a handsome lanky man named Samuel with black hair much fuller than in his photo as a toddler. There were photos of the lanky man in fatigues and a camera held close. The inscription read, 'Me here in 1973, Yom Kippur, at the Golan Heights'.

'How are you today, Gloria?' Jane the nurse said as she made the bed, the clean sheets tucked under with the hospital fold and the stained sheets put in a basket for later removal.

'I'm OK, Jane.'

Jane knew the same story would be repeated because of the photos which were strewn along with the Tarot cards which Gloria read each day – for some gullible nurse, Jane thought.

'Have you ever heard of my son Samuel, the famous New York writer? He and his wife were killed in the Twin Towers on 9/11.'

Jane just nodded, still fixing up the pillows. Jane had been a non-believer ever since her friend was abused once by an Anglican priest. She could not stop the words coming out. 'Actually, he was your nephew yesterday. Which is he today? Son or nephew?'

'You're arrogant and rude at times, Jane, and you should hear what I'm going to say.'

Jane felt a trifle ashamed and blushed but never apologised for the remark.

'I've done your cards. Two major arcanas keep coming up. The death card and the hanged man. Not death, but some changes. To balance this is a six of cups, which always means you should return to an old skill. And the old skill is cooking for your family.'

'So what about the first cards?'

Gloria hesitated yet blurted out after thinking deeply, 'Your son Jamie, isn't it? Go to the hospital now. He's there. His head is aching. Go now, Jane. But he won't die.'

Jane ran out in a panic and told a friend. She drove off towards the hospital near the school and rang on the mobile at the same time.

Her husband Claude was there, anxiously waiting. He stood up. 'They're operating right now. It's a brain tumour but they think it's benign. We just have to wait.'

'Can I see him now?'

Claude shook his head so they waited till the doctor came out. He was smiling and they both had the same thought: that's encouraging

'It's benign. He'll be OK.'

Jane felt a sudden dizziness come on her and her legs buckled. She was given a hot drink.

'Take me back to the home. I want to speak to old Gloria…and thank her.' She explained why on the return. Jane thought about the prediction and how accurate it was. She thought it had come from somewhere, maybe God, and decided she would return to a church and in that silent place get on her knees and thank God or whoever put the skill into Gloria's head to give out messages. Accurate faultless messages.

She strode straight into her room and saw the artefacts had been removed. She ran down the passage to the supervisor's office and without knocking barged in. She knew what the words would be in reply to her enquiry.

'Sorry, Jane. She died straight after you left. But she left this for you.'

Jane wiped away the tears and opened the bag. The newspaper

reports from 1973 and 9/11 fell out and she read them. Gloria was right. They were both killed in the Twin Towers.

The pack of Tarot cards was a gift as well.

Jane decided she would research all of the material and maybe later become a reader herself.

She walked back to the car and explained it all to Claude and she whispered to herself, 'You will not be forgotten, Gloria – I will be a reader. And once again a good cook to my family.'

Postscript

9/11

We knew about terror in Australia in 2001. Why wouldn't we? After all, our soldiers were engaged in other lands, giving medical aid repairing, rebuilding shattered communities, de-activating old bombs and sinking bores to provide precious clean water.

Terror struck us with the Bali bombings, well before 9/11, so only fools and those in denial thought we would remain immune and isolated. Yet it has not touched our mainland.

It all changed on 11 September 2001, when we watched with horror the attacks on New York city, a devastation which should never be forgotten.

My memories have never dimmed about that event because my wife and I saw first-hand the effect it had on many New York citizens who like us had just alighted from the 125-year-old A10 steam locomotive at Kuranda.

Kuranda is a beautiful location set high above Cairns in north Queensland, with a winding feat of railway engineering which amazed the world with its construction – as well as a chairlift for a return journey. Our carriage was full of people of many nationalities but mainly people from the United States of America and sprinkled amongst those folk were many New York citizens.

We wandered around the huge gift shop until we heard the sounds of televisions blasting out dramatic messages. The sights were scenes of great tragedies. Ann held a sobbing black young woman tightly who buried her sobbing face into my wife's shoulders. Many collapsed on the floor. The screams and tears shattered the already broken atmosphere in the gift store. I watched as a group of New York Jewish people formed a circle. Some broke the circle by holding their arms up in the air, no doubt praying to God. And the TVs continued replaying over and over the giant plane hitting the towers, the falling citizens preferring to plunge than to burn, and the white dust covering the brave emergency workers as they tried to make sense of it all.

My return journey on the ski lift was a solemn affair. We just didn't speak. We knew, though, on that day, that the planet was shaken and would never ever be the same again in our lifetime .

A galvanised resolve flooded the USA like a giant tentacle from some prehistoric sea and those tentacles wormed into every fissure on our earth. The stability which we knew, had always taken for granted, was gone.

Yet the courage of New York's citizens shone above in spite of the huge loss of life. The people of the Big Apple were never short on courage.